COMPOSITION FOR
FOUR HANDS

Also by Hilda Lawrence

Blood Upon The Snow
Death of a Doll
The House
The Pavillion
A Time to Die

COMPOSITION FOR FOUR HANDS

HILDA LAWRENCE

CUTTING EDGE

ISBN-13: 978-1-954840-18-8

Published by
Cutting Edge Books
PO Box 8212
Calabasas, CA 91372
www.cuttingedgebooks.com

To Maggie Cousins

PART ONE

THEY wheeled her chair to the big bay window in her bedroom. She'd been fed and bathed. She'd had what they called
her forty winks. They said it was a beautiful afternoon and wasn't
she lucky to have such a nice window? Then they left her. It was
Saturday. She knew it was Saturday, because school-children
were playing in the little park across the way and the florist had
come with her weekend roses. She'd bought the house because of
that little park. Nice for a child. The park and the big, rambling
gardens. For swings and play-houses, later for tennis courts .... It
was Saturday. Ralph, her husband, was home from the bank, and
he'd helped with her lunch, spooning the broth so carefully, calling her his little baby. Not speaking to her, though; to the nurse.
He'd said: "Miss Sills, she's all I've got now. She's my little baby
girl, and she's all I've got."

Miss Sills had looked as if she had wanted to cry. Her hand
had gone out as if she had wanted to touch his beautiful white
hair. She had said: "You mustn't brood, Mr. Manson. No matter
how miserable you are, you must make yourself look happy for
her sake. She's terribly sensitive, she feels things."

She could hear things, too. Sometimes they forgot that.
When they spoke directly to her, they raised their voices and
made gestures, as if she were deaf. But when they talked among
themselves, they acted as if she weren't there. They seemed to
think she couldn't hear unless they put their faces close to hers
and waved their hands. That was all right; she wanted them
to talk among themselves. The more they talked like that, the

1

better. When they left the room, she wanted to know where they were going. She wanted to know where they were every hour of the day. And the night. The night.

They left her, and she heard their footsteps going down the hall; Ralph's turned at the rose guestroom. That was where he slept now. She'd heard the doctor tell him to sleep there, to be within call. Whose call? Not hers; she couldn't open her mouth. She could open it, but she couldn't make a sound. The nurse's call. Miss Sills'.

Miss Sills had a cot at the foot of her big bed. If Miss Sills called to him in the night, he could be there in less than a minute, down the hall or across the sleeping porch that ran along that side of the house. I suppose they talk among themselves, downstairs, and say that I may die in the night, she thought. I wonder if I can smile. I don't know, they never bring me a mirror. They never put my chair anywhere near a mirror. But if I can smile, then that's what I'm doing now inside. Careful. Be careful.

MISS SILLS' footsteps went beyond the rose room to the head of the stairs, went down, and were lost in the thick rugs of the lower hall. Going for her afternoon exercise. Soon I'll hear the front door close, and then she'll wave to me from the garden. Then I'll see her across the street, in the little park, walking with long, easy steps, swinging her arms. Beautiful, beautiful motion. And pretty soon Emma will come in to sit, chirping and smiling and talking. Talking, talking, talking. But I'm used to Emma. She's been with me so long she's almost like a member of the family. She will tell me about the prices of things, pretending I still keep house. The butcher, the fruit man, the farmer with his wagon— robbers all, but what can a person do? And Emma will say: "My, but you look fine today. There's color in your cheeks."

Rouge. Miss Sills had put it on. You couldn't stop her. Rouge and curling irons and manicures. She said it was good for morale. *Morale.*

Emma would sit in the low chair, neat as a pin in her afternoon uniform, and talk about tea and dinner. And she'd have her tatting. Emma did tatting now. She used to knit, but they made her stop—because of the needles. The needles were the right shape, as nearly the right shape and size as anything could be, anything you'd be lucky enough to get your hands on. Lucky enough if your hands, if only your hands—

Hands. Emma's old hands, worn and rough because she made her living with them, but strong. Emma's old hands that didn't need strength, gripping the lovely needles. Rolling them between her fingers, turning them over and over; beautiful, beautiful motion, wasted on Emma.

Emma must have seen her watching the needles; she must have seen a look in her eyes, because she'd said, "No, no, Miss Nora, you mustn't think of such a terrible thing." Emma couldn't possibly know what she really was thinking, nobody could know. Nobody except—no, that wasn't possible. Or was it? She'd wondered and worried, driven herself half-crazy, until she overheard them talking when they thought she was asleep. Miss Sills said: "She wanted Emma's needles today. Emma saw the look. I don't like that, Mr. Manson, I don't like it at all. She couldn't hold them even if we put them in her hands—she can't even hold a hankie, not yet, not now. But I don't like it. In these cases you sometimes get a sudden change—temporary, of course, like a muscular spasm. She could do herself a serious injury if she got hold of anything like that, anything with a point. So I told Emma to stop the knitting and work on something else. Like tatting. You can't hurt yourself with a little celluloid bobbin."

He said: "Hurt herself? How dreadful! But I'm afraid you're right. I saw her watching your pencil when you were writing the drugstore list. She wanted it, she craved it. A pencil! What could she do with a pencil?"

"I don't know. We can't get into her poor mind. But really, Mr. Manson, we've got to be alert every minute. We've got to prepare ourselves for a physical change. You know she could put her—I hate to say this—she could put her—well, she could hurt her eyes. In the state she's in, I mean her emotional state, she may think of herself as useless, a burden to you. A self-inflicted injury—oh, it's too awful, the poor thing! Maybe she doesn't even want to *see!*"

His warm hands covered her then. He said: "Guard her, Miss Sills, don't let anything happen. She's all I have. Those lovely eyes, have you noticed how they—follow? They're the only thing about her that's alive."

THAT was why Emma gave up knitting for tatting, which she hated. That was why Miss Sills no longer wore pencil and pen clipped to her apron bib. A self-inflicted injury.... Don't think about it, she told herself. You're lucky, you're very lucky, because they guessed wrong. Think of something else, make yourself think, hard, hard. Think of your hands, your fingers; think of a substitute for a pencil. Anything, anything that will turn and roll between useless fingers, turn and roll and give them strength. Secret strength that must be kept hidden. If you were a soldier in a hospital, they'd put something in your hands and help you turn and roll it. In a hospital they'd help you. That's why you're not in a hospital, that's why you're home. You heard them: "She'll be more comfortable in her own home with the people she loves." Self-inflicted injury; you heard that, too. You're lucky again because you can't laugh. You're lucky because if you once started, you couldn't stop. You'd give yourself away. Self-inflicted injury, when all you want to do is to keep your life, not lose it. Keep it, such as it is, keep it until—Why, I'm crying. Those are tears on my hands. I didn't know I could cry. Think of something else. Quick.... Bruce will be coming on the four-fifteen. Better not think of that, either. Every afternoon, bending down to look into your face, kissing your hands, telling you how well you look, teasing, pretending.... Stop that. Stop that.

Look at the fringe on your steamer rug. Old, happy rug; kind, thick fringe. Thick! Almost as thick as a pencil! Try it, try it while you're alone, hurry before—before Emma comes. Before anyone comes. Before they all come tramping back from their walks, their exercise, from the station. There, you almost did it that time. Almost. But don't worry because it seems impossible now; someday you'll make it. Try. Try again. There's a good thick strand, lying across your left wrist. See if you can touch it with your other hand. See if you can move your wrist, your arm, your arm, try.... No. No, but don't cry again, that's getting you nowhere. Keep trying, and thank God your mind is all right. That's what they aren't sure of, your mind. That's where you're ahead of them; that's how you'll win in the end. One of these days one of your hands will reach the fringe and close over it. One of these days you will take the fringe in your hand and open and close your fingers. Roll the soft, thick fringe between your fingers, endlessly, over and over, until they are strong enough to hold a pencil. Pencil. You'll never even see another pencil. You know that. But your fingers will be ready for whatever comes. It doesn't matter if you never walk again, if you never speak again. All you need is two fingers. Two? No, one. One will be enough, one finger can point. You can pretend to be writing with one finger, a pantomime. You can make it clear and unmistakable if you are ever alone with the right person .... But how will I know which person is right? I'm not sure even now. How will I know which one is both right and safe? Now, now, don't cry. It takes away the little strength you have. Now, now, don't be a baby. "My little baby girl," he said .... There's Emma.

MILLY SILLS crossed the park and hurried to the Larchville station. The four-fifteen from New York was pulling in, and the platform was filled with families and dogs. She had time only to set her beret becomingly awry before George Perry and Mr. Bruce Cory came shouldering through the crowd. Milly and George, who lived, with his father and mother, next door to the Mansons', had been friends for some time. She eyed Mr. Cory rather hostilely, but had to admit he was a handsome devil for—what was it, fifty? Emma had told her that the other Mr. Cory, Mrs. Manson's first husband, had been about ten years older than Mrs. Manson, and she was forty-two. And Bruce Cory was that Mr. Cory's twin. Well, handsome devil for fifty-two or whatever it was. No fat, not an ounce. He made old George look like a puppy.

"Damn," Milly said under her breath, "it looks as if George and I can't be alone for even five minutes these days." She waved, and they waved over the other commuters' heads. She made rapid plans for the evening. Maybe a movie, maybe dancing, maybe both. "I'll work on him," she decided. "I don't care if he does look grim. He'll have to get over that. I, for one, won't have it. I, for one, am having too much as it is."

However, she noted, there was nothing grim about Bruce Cory, with the polo-field skin and the squash-court figure. She watched his approach with admiration and appropriate distrust. He walked as if he had oiled hinges.

"Mr. Perry, I believe," she said to George when they came up to her. She hooked an affectionate arm through George's and gave him a pinch, but he didn't seem to feel it. To Bruce Cory she gave the smile she kept in reserve for patients' relatives.

"Hi," George said. "I ran into Mr. Cory in the smoker."

Cory returned her smile with a look of approval that traveled from her white canvas shoes to her white beret. She felt herself liking it. George had given her one look, a quick one, with absolutely nothing in it. But nothing.

They moved across the platform. "Cab or walk?" George asked.

"Walk," she said. "This is my airing."

Cory was instantly solicitous, looking down with a worried air. "Are you having any fun?" he asked. "Or is it all perfectly deadly?"

Having any fun, she jeered silently. What a thing to say! I know you, my friend. To date you've given no trouble, but there's one of your kind on every case.... She gave him the smile she kept in reserve for that kind, the one that said: "When I go downstairs at midnight in my bathrobe, I'm going for hot cocoa—get it? Cocoa." Aloud, "Everything's fine, Mr. Cory, thank you," she said.

"Anything happen after I left this morning? Any change?"

"No change. No change is considered fine in cases like this. We can't ask for more than that for a while. But she had a good lunch—good for her, I mean—and she seems to be making an effort in other ways, too."

"Splendid! What kind of effort?"

"Well, she seems to notice things. I haven't said much about it except to Mr. Manson, but I do feel encouraged. I think she's trying to concentrate. You know, listen. She seems to realize that she's helpless, and her eyes—"

Cory spoke sharply. "What about her eyes?"

"Oh, nothing like that, Mr. Cory!" He did love her, they all did. In her way she was lucky. Some people had no one, had to go to city hospitals and wear dark, shapeless robes all day long because they didn't show the dirt or the food that got spilled. Mrs. Manson had real silk and fine wool, and there wasn't a single minute when somebody wasn't trying to anticipate her wants, read her thoughts. Read her thoughts—if she had any. That was something they weren't sure about.

"Oh, no, Mr. Cory, there's nothing wrong with her vision. I only mean she notices more and tries to watch everything we do, although she can't turn her head, not yet. But I'm pretty sure she'll be able to do that soon. I even told Mr. Manson so." Then, because Mr. Cory still looked unhappy and unconvinced, she added: "Cheer up. It could be worse. Think how poor Mr. Manson feels."

Cory nodded. "Good little Sills," he said. "We were lucky to get you."

They walked on in silence.

TONIGHT she would be free from eight to twelve. Once a week she had a night like that. Sometimes she went home, a fifteen-minute walk across town, lugging a suitcase of laundry for her mother to do. It wasn't necessary, but her mother liked to do it. Her mother always met her at the front door and took the suitcase before she kissed her. She dumped the clothes into the washing machine as if she were fighting a plague. Then she sat in the rocker she kept in the kitchen and double-dared anybody to come within a yard of the machine. The washer was a Christmas present from Milly, and the capable, elderly maid was a present, too. But Mrs. Sills chose to regard the washer as her own invention and the maid as an indigent relative, not right in the head. "Maybe I ought to go home," Milly thought. "I missed last week." Then she looked at George. Still grim. A face like granite. Jealous, she gloated. What do you know! Her heart suddenly warmed. "Movies tonight, George?"

"Not tonight."

"What's the matter with you?"

"Toothache."

"Of course you've seen the dentist?"

"No."

"Well, of course you will, won't you?"

"Maybe."

Fool, she thought. Why do I bother? Suit yourself, lie awake all night and suffer. See if I care …. Later, when she remembered that, she felt as if she'd been daring an ax to fall on her neck. Because George didn't go to the dentist, and he did lie awake. He got up at three in the morning to spit a poultice out the window, and she cared a great deal.

Now Cory was saying something and she turned with elaborate interest. "I beg your pardon, Mr. Cory. I didn't get that."

"I asked you what you thought of Doctor Babcock," Cory said carelessly.

"I have every confidence in Doctor Babcock," she said primly. "So has Mr. Manson."

"I know he has. Babcock's the only one who's lasted. I understand you've worked with him before?"

It was a question, not a statement. She was pleased. He doesn't know how green I am, she thought. I must be doing all right. Maybe none of them knows.... Her reply was short but lofty. "Oh, my, yes." One tonsillectomy.

She remembered the night, a little less than two weeks before, when Doctor Babcock had routed her out of bed. He didn't tell her what the case was, and she turned it down, because she'd just wound up six weeks with a simple fracture, age twelve, who slept all day and demanded comics all night. She said she needed sleep. But he told her he was desperate, his patient was unhappy with her present nurse. He was perfectly frank; he admitted the woman was difficult and would probably be unhappy with Florence Nightingale. It was like Babcock to drag in Nightingale. Then he'd said the patient was Mrs. Manson. At that, she'd gone with him, at once, at one o'clock in the morning.

She'd been glad of her decision ever since, and it had nothing to do with the fact that good old George's house was practically in the Manson back yard. Mrs. Manson liked her, she could see that. And Babcock looked pleased. That meant a lot. Her first really important case. If she made good, there wouldn't be any more spoiled kids and old women. If she made good, she could stay with Mrs. Manson until the end. The end? Well, stay until something happened one way or another. Or until Milly herself couldn't take it.

"What did Babcock say this morning?" Cory was pressing her arm.

"He didn't come, Mr. Cory. He called up right after you left. He said he'd drop in this afternoon. I don't like to be away when he comes, even when Mr. Manson and Emma are there, but if I don't go out at my regular hours, I get dopey. And that's not good for Mrs. Manson."

"What about another nurse? I don't know why we haven't insisted on that."

"Not a chance. I suggested it myself, and if you'd seen the look in her eyes—She's terrified of people, even old friends who come to inquire. We've had to stop all that. We have to be awfully careful, even with the people in the house. Like Hattie, the cook. The cook's all right when she keeps her mouth shut, but the other day she burst into tears and talked about Mrs. Manson's son."

"About Robbie?" At her nod, Cory looked away. "Bad," he said.

"Bad? It was criminal. George was there; he saw the whole thing. But we didn't tell a soul. No use getting Hattie fired. We simply gave her—we laid her out. She won't do that again."

"You can tell me about it, can't you? Forget that I'm Robbie's uncle."

She answered eagerly, appealing to George, forcing him into the conversation. "Of course we can tell Mr. Cory, can't we, George? You do it; you know the background better than I do. You see, I didn't know about Robbie's birthday, Mr. Cory. How could I? If I'd known, I'd have got Hattie out the minute she started. Tell it, George."

George complied, slowly and reluctantly. "It isn't much," he said. "But it was a nuisance. You know I'm in and out of the house a lot these days, at odd hours. And you know I practically lived in the place when I was a kid. Mrs. Manson never let them fill in the hedge."

Cory said, "Yes, I know." He knew that the Perry cottage backed on the Manson garden, and that the dividing hedge still showed gaps made by small boys in a hurry. He knew all about the childhood friendship and that George was a few years older than Robbie, and that after they outgrew the swings, the play-houses, and the gym apparatus, they didn't see much of each other.

"We went with different crowds when we grew up," George said. "Naturally. You know how that happens. This last year I hardly ever saw him. He was twenty-one and I was twenty-six—that makes a lot of difference. To say nothing of Robbie's unlimited money." In spite of himself he emphasized money.

"Forget that," Cory said. "Go on with your story."

ACCORDING to George, his mother said it would be nice if he began to hang around the Mansons again—second-son stuff. And Mrs. Manson seemed to like it. At least, he said, she didn't have a relapse. Not until the Hattie episode. He'd been dropping in for several weeks when that happened, having drinks in Mrs. Manson's room, talking about anything that came into his head, never mentioning Robbie. Nothing ever upset her when he was there alone, even though he was pretty sure she didn't hear half he said. She just looked at him, accepted him, and that was all anybody hoped for. Then the cook business happened.

"Small thing in its way," George said, "but a fine example of the chances you take when you don't control the people who go to see her."

He said he'd been doing his usual routine that afternoon, rambling on about the weather, the pretty sky, and see how the leaves are turning, Mrs. Manson. Thanksgiving on the way, Halloween before you know it, and so on. Then Hattie came in with a lamb chop and a piece of chicken on a plate. Raw. A custom of the house, a scheme to coax Mrs. Manson into thinking. Emma's idea. Here are two pieces of meat. You may have one for your dinner. Which? Emma swore it worked; she said Hattie could tell which one Mrs. Manson wanted by the way she looked.

George said he had reached Halloween in his therapeutic travelogue, pumpkin faces, and so on, when Hattie burst into tears and started to babble.

"I was sunk," George said. "I'd forgotten that Robbie's birthday was all tied up with pumpkins. But Hattie hadn't. She carried on about the jack-o'-lanterns they used to put in his room on birthdays. They did that from the time he was three until he was eighteen. Then he made them stop it. Did you know that?"

"Yes," Cory said. "They all babied him."

"Exactly," George agreed. "Well, that's all, but it sent Mrs. Manson right up to the taking off place and turned me into an old man. Hattie still comes in with her plate of raw meat, but she doesn't talk."

The little park was straight ahead, and across the park the big house stood in its bright fall garden. Milly thought of the motionless figure she had left by the window, and her steps dragged. She listened half-heartedly to the conversation. They were getting along all right without her; George was warming up, for him. Giving out information instead of hoarding it, treating Cory like an equal. Now he was saying something in a soft voice about a dreamy kid.

"Always was," George said. "Always lived in another world. Robbie had his mother's features, but he didn't have her—excitement. Of course, I never saw his father; but taking you as a model, I'd say Robbie wasn't like a Cory, either."

It was an obvious compliment, George's voice was deferential and admiring, and Cory flushed. Milly said to herself, "Good old George, he'll get a job out of Cory yet."

"When my brother died," Cory said quietly, "I rather hoped she'd remarry. I was glad when she did. No, Robbie wasn't like my brother. Robbie was—himself."

George said: "I don't like to think about it. I don't even like to talk about it."

BUT Milly thought about it as they entered the park and crossed under the yellow maples, between flaming beds of scarlet sage. The maple leaves were gold, the gold of new coin. A boy with all the money in the world, with anything— "Do you think they'll ever find out what he did with it?" she asked vaguely.

Cory didn't answer. He said, "Is she in her window?"

"She should be," she told him. "We put her there as usual, Mr. Manson and I, just before I came out. She likes to watch the park—at least, I think she does. I told Emma not to touch her, to wait until I came back. It's sort of queer—" She stopped to challenge her own words and to wonder why they suddenly asked for challenge.

"What's queer?" Cory was smiling. "The window? Or Emma?"

She answered slowly. "Neither. I only mean she's funny about being touched. I don't think she likes it, and we're pretty sure it isn't a question of pain. But when I get back from my walks and go to her room, I always feel as if she's been waiting for me. For *me*. Almost—well, anxiously. And I've only been on the case a little while; it isn't as if I were an old friend. I guess it's the uniform. People seem to trust nurses." I've said something idiotic, she told herself instantly. Cory had given her a quick, sharp look, and George was rolling his eyes to heaven. As if I'd pulled a boner, she thought, as if I were feeble-minded. I'll show them.

"And the more fools they," she said briskly. "I mean, for trusting nurses. I can count cases on all ten fingers that would curl your hair. Helpless patient plus renegade husband, son, brother, doctor, lawyer, friend. Take your choice. Willing female confederate, uniform from a theatrical place. Object, money. And believe me—" She stopped again, appalled. Why don't you pack up and get out before you're fired? she mourned to herself.

"Brilliant girl," George said to Cory. "And simply crazy about Mill Sills, R.N."

They turned in at the gate.

MRS. MANSON was still by the window. She'd seen them turn into the park and cross, talking.

Emma had seen them, too. "There, now," Emma said, "there's Mr. Brucie and George Perry with Miss Sills. I'd say she went to the station to meet them, wouldn't you?" Emma smiled and nodded and waved. She looked as if she were glad to see someone who could smile and wave in return. And talk. Poor Emma. Talking, talking, talking, and never being quite sure that she was heard.

"You're lucky, that's what you are," Emma insisted. "And I want you to remember it, and appreciate it. A nice young girl like Miss Sills to look after you. A daughter couldn't do more. And Mr. Bruce Cory, giving up his beautiful New York apartment to come out here and cheer you up, for old times' sake. Giving up his gay city life, when we all know he hates the country. He's popular, too, he is. In the gossip columns nearly every day, but in a nice way. No café society for Mr. Brucie; he runs with the cream dee lah cream."

She stopped listening to Emma. There were other things to listen to.

The front door opened, and they walked across the strip of floor that was bare. Then they walked on the rugs. Then the sound of their voices. Ralph's voice, low, greeting them. Then another door, the library. They were going to have a drink before they all came up, trooping in full of smiles. "How wonderful you look! You keep this up, and you'll be out for Christmas!" Out? Out where? Out beside Robbie.

Doctor Babcock encouraged them to talk like that. He himself talked like that, rocking back and forth on his strong legs. They all did that, rocked; they thought it made them look as if they had nothing on their minds. But she'd seen the look Babcock had given Ralph the day before. She'd been keeping her eyes almost closed, as children do when they pretend to be asleep, looking between her lashes. Babcock had looked at Ralph and shaken his head. Hopeless, the look had said. And he'd shrugged and raised his eyebrows in answer to an unspoken question of Ralph's. The shrug and brows said, "Hopeless, except for a miracle."

They were all watching for a miracle, for a sign of change. She saw it in their faces, heard it in their voices. They knew what to watch for; they discussed its improbability as if she were already dead. And one of them knew how much that kind of talk meant to her. One of the people who came to her room was quietly alert, lying in wait for a sign that showed she understood. She had read the speculation in one pair of eyes. She was much cleverer than that; she was careful to let her own eyes show nothing. If the miracle came, she knew she must hide it. The first sign of a twitch, the first small movement, one finger, one muscle in her body, and the news would go all over the house, over the town. And that would be the end of her. "Have you heard about Mrs. Manson? Too bad, just when she was beginning to show improvement." Maybe it would happen before that. In a panic, in a sudden panic—

She looked at the rug, at the fringe lying across her knees. She looked at it until her eyes burned. "Emma," she implored silently, "Emma—"

"Now, what's wrong with your nice rug?" Emma scolded. "I declare, you're looking as if you wanted to eat it up! Could that mean you're cold? No, your face is nice and warm. Let Emma feel your hands. So that's it, hands freezing. Well, we'll tuck them in a little wool nest. There you are. Oh, my poor Miss Nora. Oh, my poor lady."

The hands were covered, that was luck again. Or was it something else? Was she projecting her thoughts, making Emma think what she wanted her to think? Good, simple, childish Emma and her good, simple mind. Could her own mind possibly direct Emma's? Concentrate! If you can do that, who knows what may happen? If you can will Emma to come and go, you may have a minute alone. A minute alone when you need it. A minute alone when the time comes .... Don't think about that now, she's watching you. Close your eyes. Somebody said the eyes are windows of the soul. If that's true, close them.

The thick fringe, the good thick fringe, was in the palm of one hidden hand. She closed her eyes and dreamed about it lying there, afraid to try anything stronger than a dream.

THEY came in, all four of them, through the door that was beyond the half-circle of her vision, all four and a fifth. Ralph, Brucie, George Perry, Miss Sills, and another one. A strange one. She closed a door in her mind; she'd been away on a journey of her own, crawling inch by inch, even walking, in her dream world. When they filed across the room and stood in a line before her chair, she saw who the fifth one was. Doctor Babcock. She made herself look down at his feet, she could just manage it, turning her eyes down until they hurt. He was wearing overshoes. That was why she hadn't known his muffled tread. It was raining, then. Yes, it was growing dark outside, there was rain on the windows.

Miss Sills said brightly: "We're going to have a little party. As soon as George builds up the fire. See, here's George! He says he wants a drink, but we're going to make him work for it. And here's another man—picked me up at the station, he did, claiming he lives here now. Shall we give him a drink, too?"

Miss Sills was flushed and happy. *She's in love with one of them. Which?*

Ralph had a tray, and he put it on the tea cart that held the medicine and rubbing oils, the strong glass feeding tube, the lipstick, the firm, cylindrical lipstick. A tray of drinks. One for her? There was a rattle of coal in the grate, then a sound of smothered laughter. Miss Sills and George. It was George she loved.

Brucie bent to kiss her cheek. "How's our baby?" He drew her hands from beneath the rug and massaged them gently, smiling down into her face. "We started to have drinks downstairs, and then Ralph got this idea. Babcock came in and said it was okay. See the glass of milk? Look. Funny color." He took it from the tray and held it before her. "Milk plus. The plus is rum. Good for girls."

The fringe was lying across her knees, wasting its beautiful potentialities.

Doctor Babcock didn't wait for the others. He took his drink, raised it in a toast to the rest, and gulped half of it. "Good for boys," he said.

They laughed. Even Emma. Emma said, "Doctor, you never give me any medicine like that!" They laughed again, and Emma's shrill cackle rose above the rich, masculine rumbles and the light, applauding ripple that nurses always save for doctors.

Ralph handed the drinks around, Scotch and soda in the hunting-scene glasses. The glasses she'd bought at Tiffany's six weeks before. Only six weeks? Only that? The day she had lunch with Robbie at the Plaza. The day—

RALPH's strong brown hand held the milk close to her mouth. His other hand held the feeding tube. He said: "No dreaming, darling, this is a party. For you. Now take a nice long swallow for the old man."

She closed her lips, made them tight.

He coaxed. "Come, darling, it's good. Bruce made it himself. See? I'll take a swallow first."

Brucie's face, full of mock chagrin. His laughing voice. "What's the idea—testing for poison?"

Awful, awful, awful to say a thing like that. To say it out loud, to make a joke of it. To say it, to say it.

Miss Sills, crossing the room rapidly, coming to her chair. "Hey!" Miss Sills, rattling off a long sentence, addressing them all, meaningless words ending with the same letters. Pig Latin. Robbie used to—Pig Latin.

Miss Sills was telling them not to say things like that. Miss Sills was all right. Watch Miss Sills closely, make sure. If Miss Sills is all right, then—

They both took her hands, Ralph and Brucie.

"Baby," Ralph said, "forgive us. We're clumsy fools. You've always been such a good sport, we sometimes forget we must be careful now. You understand?"

Brucie kissed the hand he held and placed it on top of the rug. On top. He took the milk from Ralph. "Let me," he said. He slipped the feeding tube between her lips.

The drink was all right. It tasted good. Rum and milk. Nothing else, simply rum and milk with a little grated nutmeg. She should have known there would be nothing else. Poison would be ridiculous, unintelligent.

Emma fussed with her sewing basket and said she was going. "Going to see that the table's set properly. Doctor Babcock's having dinner with us. He invited himself when they told him it was steak. You're going to have steak, too, a special treat. I'll cut it up myself, nice and fine. Nice and rare, to build you up. What do you want, Miss Nora? Oh, dear, tell Emma what it is you want? I can feel you asking."

Concentrate. Hard, hard. The rug, the rug over your hands, both hands. The fringe.

They all watched, they crowded her chair, looking at her, at Emma, at one another.

Doctor Babcock said, "Emma, I'm afraid you'll have to go unless you—"

Emma crowed. "I know! Don't tell me what I'm to do and what not to do! It's her hands! See how she looks at them? She likes them covered up, wrapped up in that old rug. I found that out this afternoon, and I'm no doctor. They get cold, no activity, you might say. It stands to reason—you don't need college to know that. There you are, my pretty girl, my smart, pretty girl!"

She closed her eyes because the relief was almost unbearable. It works, I can make her do what I want her to do. The fringe was thick and firm between her hidden fingers. Look as if you were sleeping, look as if you were sleeping, and concentrate.

"Wheel her chair to the fire, and leave her alone for a bit." Emma, firm and arrogant with success. "She'll be happy by the fire and knowing you're all with her. No loud talk and laughing, mind you, none of your wicked jokes. Surrounded by her loved ones, all cozy and warm, that's what she needs."

Miss Sills: "Who's the nurse around here? Let me see your credentials, madam."

Soft laughter. Her chair moving forward, the warmth increasing, the door closing on Emma, the hushed regrouping of other chairs, the crack of coal in the grate, the ring of ice cubes against glass. Low voices talking about football. She didn't have to listen to that. She could travel back and pick up the threads. The threads would make a tapestry, and the tapestry would show the figures.

THE day she bought the glasses with the hunting scenes, Fifth Avenue was all the world's great streets in one; the day was all September days together. She remembered to put a bag of cracked corn in her purse for St. Patrick's pigeons, and she sent her car to a garage, because she wanted to walk. Once she saw her reflection in a window and preened like a girl. "I look thirty," she said to herself, "and why not? All the other women have only painted faces and lovers, but I have Ralph and Robbie."

It was too early for lunch. Robbie couldn't make it until one. That was ridiculous, and she'd told Ralph so; when a bank is practically a family business, it ought to make concessions to the young squire. But Robbie wouldn't have it that way. She'd asked him once why he worked so hard, and he'd said it was because he hated it. "You have a frightful conscience," she'd said. "You got it from me, you poor thing, but I'll make it up to you."

Walking up Fifth Avenue, she planned a surprise. She'd tell him he needn't stay at the bank after the first of the year. By that time Ralph and Brucie would know he wasn't lazy. She'd tell him he could go abroad and write. These youngsters who wanted to write! It was the Left Bank or sterility. No good telling them they were wrong, no good telling them that a kitchen table in Brooklyn and a stack of paper are all a writer needs.

McCutcheon's. Dinner napkins. Big heavy, luscious dinner napkins with fat, rich monograms. She didn't need them, she had too many, and hardly anyone used them any more. But square, solid piles of damask carefully wrapped in muslin and reaching to the top of the closet shelf, that was a beautiful sight. And practical in case you felt like giving a buffet supper for a couple of hundred people. You might feel like that. For instance, you might have a wedding. She ordered two dozen.

Tiffany's. Just to look around, that's all. Everybody did that. Look around like a tourist, ogle the diamonds. Beautiful diamonds, solitaires, very practical in case you had an—She hurried to the floor where the glassware was, struggling to keep her face straight, and ordered three dozen highball glasses with hunting scenes. Practical if you felt like giving a hunt breakfast. No, that's champagne. Or doesn't it matter? It does. She ordered the champagne glasses, too.

The Plaza. The hacks, the coachmen, one old fellow with a wilted orchid pinned to his coat. Some girl last night, some pretty young thing with her best beau, jogging through Central Park. Maybe the girl got engaged; maybe she gave it to him and told him to wear it for luck.

The waiter captain. Robbie had phoned that he'd be a little late and she wasn't to wait. The captain gave her the message. "Mrs. Manson, Mr. Cory said you were to go ahead. He suggested a nice old-fashioned."

SHE ordered the drink. One-fifteen, one-twenty. Then she knew he was there even before he bent over the back of her chair and kissed her neck. Demonstrative, for Robbie.

"Toper," he said.

"Robbie!" He looked dreadful. "Robbie, what have you been doing to yourself?"

"Working for your living. Why?" He rubbed a hand over his face. "Maybe I forgot to shave."

"You did not! Robbie, if I positively didn't know you were in your own bed at ten, I'd say you'd spent the night in sin. Tell me what's wrong. Don't lie to me, tell me!"

He said he was tired, that was all. Tired, so help him. "Do you want me to cross my heart in a joint like this?" He wouldn't look at her. He ordered his lunch without the menu; shirred eggs, black coffee. Drink? No, no drink.

She talked, talked her head off, told him about the new napkins, the new glasses; but he wasn't listening. He was sick, he must be dreadfully sick. "Robbie, where does it hurt? Now, don't be childish. You've got a pain somewhere, and I want to know. It can't be your appendix, that's out. What *have* you got left? I always forget which of yours came out and which of mine. No tonsils, no appendix, no—no—Robbie, your heart!"

"I still have that," he assured her. And he laughed; too loud, too sharp. He parried every personal allusion and kept the conversation on her weakness for linen and crystal, her transportation of cracked com from Larchville in a Bergdorf bag, when she could buy a paper sack of it from a little man who hung around the cathedral for that very purpose.

She gave up. She'd get him alone that night; she'd go to his room whether he liked it or not; she'd make him tell her what was wrong. "Home for dinner, Robbie?"

"You bet."

That was all, He phoned for her car and waited until it came. He handed her in and strode off, across the street, into Central Park.

"NORA, we're going down to dinner, darling. Miss Sills will stay until Emma comes." Ralph.

"No roller-skating in the halls, baby. It's bad for the carpet." Brucie.

"Lucky Mrs. Manson, to be able to sleep so gracefully. You're better, my dear lady, I know it, I can see it, I've been waiting for it. I think I'll speak to the masseur. Perhaps we can lengthen the treatments. If I had your fine spirit and this charming room, I wouldn't mind a touch of invalidism myself!" Dr. Babcock.

"Thanks for the drinks, Mrs. Manson. Good-night." George Perry.

"Thanks for getting out of here, all of you, and quick." Miss Sills.

"That's right, slam the door. Deliver me from men in a sick-room!" Miss Sills again, patting her shoulder. "I thought they'd cheer you up, but you don't look too cheery. Hear me tell Babcock to get out with the others? I don't know the meaning of fear. I'll say anything. If he fires me off this case, I'll come straight back. I'll climb the ivy and crawl through the window. Baby this and baby that. Don't you make any mistake about whose baby you are. You're mine."

Miss Sills was all right, she must be, she had to be. When the time came, Miss Sills would stand fast. She was young—how young? Twenty-four or – five? But she was physically strong, and she'd been trained to think and act fast. Stand fast. Stand. At bay? No, not at bay. It wouldn't come like that. It would come in the dark, on silent feet, as it had come before. Come when she was alone. But if there were no time to lose, if minutes, even seconds, were precious, it would strike without waiting, without warning.

If it came like that, Miss Sills would have to die, too. Not Miss Sills, not a young girl who'd done nothing!

"Isn't that rug too hot now? Mrs. Manson, I think the rug's too hot with the fire going full blast. Here, let me take it. You're roasting, You look like a little red beet."

Take the rug? Take the fringe away? No! No!

"Now what have I said that's wrong? Don't you like being called a little red beet? Golly, honey—I mean, Mrs. Manson, I wish I knew what you wanted. You do want something, don't you? I wish I—say, has it something to do with your rug? Emma said you'd taken a sudden fancy to it. Did I guess right? Right! Well, then, it's yours. You keep it. I'll just move your chair back from the fire. That's better, isn't it? You know something, Mrs. Manson? One of these days you're going to smile at me, and that's the day I'm waiting for."

Dear Miss Sills. Be careful, Miss Sills. Don't be too good to me . . . .

At nine o'clock that evening Alice Perry walked into her son's room. George was reading in bed, and he looked up at her without speaking when she entered.

"Sulking, George?" Alice Perry's hair was like cotton batting, and her round face was fresh and firm. Her voice was firm also.

"No. Toothache."

"You've seen a dentist?"

"No. It'll go away."

"Sometimes you act like a child, dear. You'll find a package of those small poultices in the medicine cabinet. Use one tonight, and see a dentist in the morning. I shouldn't have to tell you that." She walked about the small room, rearranging chairs, replacing books on shelves, frowning at a bowl of yellow chrysanthemums. "Who brought these in here? You?"

"Yes, I like the color. Nothing wrong with that, is there?"

"No, of course not. But you're clumsy with flowers. These are much too stiff, and the bowl's all wrong. Never mind that now, I'll do them over tomorrow. George?"

"Yes, Mother." He put his book aside.

"You stopped there on the way home, didn't you?"

He didn't need her half-look at the windows that faced the Perry back yard, the gaping hedge, and the Manson garden. "Yes, for a little while."

"How is she?"

"Tut, tut. I can remember when you gave me the devil for saying 'she.' Like this: 'If you mean Mrs. Manson, say so.' Sure I stopped. I had a couple of drinks." He was entirely good-humored and smiling. "Mrs. Manson is the same."

"Still helpless? I mean, still dependent?" She added, "Poor creature."

"Still all of that. No speech, no movement."

"Ralph Manson tells me nothing. Bruce Cory is just as bad. I ask every day, by telephone or in person. I knew Nora Manson when she was Nora Cory. I took you to call when she moved here and Robbie was a toddler and you weren't much more. Ralph and Bruce know that as well as they know their own names. Yet sometimes I think they don't want me in the house."

"No." HE answered carefully. "You mustn't make it a personal issue. I think they feel it's better for her to see no one outside the immediate family. If she's beginning to be aware of her condition—and they think she is—why—"

"Why what, George?" She laughed. "Talked yourself into a corner that time, didn't you? *You* see her, don't you?"

"Yes. But luckily for me, my connection with the family is on a different plane. I represent bicycles in the hall, peanut butter on the piano keys, stuff like that. All very wholesome and nostalgic in the right way."

"And exactly what do I represent, you silly?" She ruffled his hair.

"Now, Mother, use your pretty little head. You're another woman, and you're healthy, and you haven't had any trouble. Also, and very important, you were there that day; if she sees you, it's bound to—upset her. They don't want that. They want her to live as she does, from hour to hour, in a sort of merciful stupor, segregated from the past. Because if she ever does get well, she'll have plenty of time to mull things over. She'll have a whole lifetime to look back on, and she won't see a pretty picture. Let her have this, whatever you call it, hiatus. If she gets well and looks back on *this,* it'll seem like heaven."

"George, you get more like your father every day. You treat me as if I didn't have good sense.... I don't think she's going to get well."

"Why not?"

"Those specialists from town. They came and went. If they'd been hopeful, we'd have heard about it. But there hasn't been a word, at least not what *I* call a word. And now there's only Babcock. She's lost her mind, hasn't she? Frankly, she never had much of one to lose."

He picked up his book and flipped over a page. If he meant it for a signal of dismissal, it wasn't heeded.

"Cat got your tongue, Georgie?" She was amused, standing by the bed, looking down and smiling.

"Toothache. No, she hasn't lost her mind."

"Then what do they call this—this state?"

"Shock and paralysis, one bound up with the other. Some cases have been cured."

"Have they? Well, I'm glad to hear it."

SHE walked to the windows, examined the chintz curtains and admired the design. "This was a good buy," she said. "I'm a good shopper." The rain fell lightly against the glass. She tapped the pane with immaculate little fingers. "Your father went to the movies. On a night like this, he must be crazy. Or bored. I asked him which, and he looked as if he couldn't decide what to answer. Funny man."

"He likes the rain," George said. "He likes to walk in it."

"The ground is soaking." She hummed and tapped the pane, peering out into the dark, dripping gardens. Then: "George, the lights are on in her room. Why, at this hour?"

"Masseur. This is the time he comes. She sleeps afterward."

"Sedatives, of course?"

"Yep." He looked up from his book, startled by the sudden sound of curtain rings traveling across the rods. "What's the idea?" he asked agreeably. "I like them the way they were. I like to look out."

"There's nothing to see."

"Sure there is. The rain. I like it, same as the old man."

"It's depressing. And there's a draft. These windows never did fit properly. Shoddy building in the first place, but what can I do? Your father's satisfied as long as the roof doesn't leak on his bed .... That girl went out a while ago, George. I saw her from the kitchen window. I think she saw me, too. She came around the side of the house and looked over here. Then she went away in a hurry."

"Name of Sills, Mother. Miss or Milly, take your choice."

"Now, George, there's absolutely no need for that frozen stare. You know how I feel. She's not—she's not your type. You've had every advantage, I've seen to that, and you can thank me for it. I honestly think it would kill me if you threw yourself away on an ordinary—"

"Easy, Mater. How do you like the Mater touch? That's my fine education." He looked contrite at once. "Listen, Ma, I've got a toothache, I don't feel like talking. Run along now, like a good egg."

"Don't think you can get around me with that 'egg.' Are you going to slip out and meet her later?"

"I hadn't thought of it, but since you've given me the idea—"

"George! I can't imagine where a girl like that goes at night. It was nearly half past eight when she left. I must say it looks very odd."

"This happens to be her night off. She usually goes home to see her mother. She's nuts about her mother. And her father, unfortunately dead and unable to speak for himself, was an honest-Injun college man. Now you know it all. So how about me bringing Miss Sills over here some afternoon? She has time off in the afternoon, too."

"Really, George!"

"Well, why not? I'll tip her off to wear the Sophie original, and you won't be able to tell her from a lady."

He was pleased when the door slammed on his last words. For a while he stayed where he was, stretching his long legs and staring at the ceiling, prodding his tender jaw with a pessimistic finger. Then he got up and went down the hall to the medicine cabinet in the bathroom.

The poultices were there—everything was always where she said it would be. He tucked one of them over his aching tooth, laughed to himself in the mirror, and returned to his room. There he drew back the curtains, raised a window, and stood looking out into the dark, wet night. Far across the stretch of gardens the lamps on the Mansons' street were a chain of dim yellow halos. There was almost no traffic; an occasional car crept warily over the shining asphalt and was lost in the blur of rain and trees and lights that marked the shopping center across the park. The rain hung like a veil a few inches before his face; he felt as if he could part it with his hand and look through to something that was now obscured.

Mrs. Manson's sleeping porch filled the center of a land-scaped vista. He remembered when she'd had that vista made. She'd said she wanted to watch them while they played. Watch him and Robbie. Two men had put ladders against the trees and swung in the branches like monkeys while she directed them from the ground. A great day for him and Robbie, with branches falling from the air and the servants running around in circles.

Now her room was bright with lights; but as he watched, they went out, one by one, until a single lamp burned. He knew that room so well that he knew where each lamp was and what it looked like. The one that was left stood on a small table by the glass door that opened onto the porch. The bulb was purposely weak. It was meant to give comfort to sleepless eyes, nothing more.

Two figures came to the glass door and stood there, a slight woman in black and a stocky man in white. He knew their silhouettes and their unvarying ritual; he didn't need their black and white for identification. Emma and the masseur; a last-minute chat, whispered amenities, compliments given and taken by two people in the pay of the same household. The masseur moved like a chimpanzee disguised as a man or a man disguised as a chimpanzee. But Milly said he was good. The best in the business, she said.

George watched the man take his leave. He could count every invisible step, every foot of the upper hall, stairway, and lower hall, and give to each its allotted time. So much for the hat-and-coat routine, so much for the walk to the front gate, so much for crossing the street to the park, for the left turn toward the station, which would bring him into view again.

His bare elbows were on the dripping windowsill and the wet wind was making his tooth jump, but he was too intent to notice. It was the final, hissing exhalation of his breath that startled him out of his absorption. What am I doing this for? he asked himself. What am I breathing heavily about?

The man, whose name was Breitman, had come into view on schedule and was moving in the right direction for the station, head lowered, trunk forward, long arms hanging wide. What am I doing this for? George asked himself again. What's the big idea of keeping tabs? The guy could have stopped for a drink with Manson and Cory—he sometimes does. So what? ... His eyes returned to the glass door. The single lamp had been moved back. Its light was as faint as the glow of a distant city reflected in the sky, but it was enough to show the passing to and fro of Emma's slight, black figure. She raised and lowered the linen shades that covered the glass panes of the door, then raised them again and opened half of the door. She disappeared and returned with a painted screen, which she dragged into place before the open section. He smiled, because he knew she was making faces and talking to herself. When Emma took charge of things, she always told herself she was the only person in the house who saw that Miss Nora got what was good for her. The screen wasn't Emma's job, it was Manson's or Cory's, even Milly's; but Emma beat them to it when she could. Once or twice he had been in the house at bedtime and tried to lend a hand; but Emma had brushed him aside and tossed him out with a few choice words. Well, he thought, tonight she's having it her way, and tomorrow the family will pay and pay. And so will I, he decided, touching his cheek and preparing to wince. But the tooth wasn't too bad; in fact, it was much better. He returned to his bed and book and settled against the pillows.

The wet wind blew in at the open window, spattering the curtains that were such a good buy. He told himself they could take it. It was good to be under the covers, in an empty room, with thoughts instead of people for company. The upstairs telephone extension rang faintly. It was at the end of the hall, outside his mother's room. He didn't notice how many times it rang; his mind was far away, across the dark, wet gardens, across the little park with its dripping trees, as far away as the Sills' cottage. When he thought of the phone again, it had stopped ringing. The whole house was silent.

EMMA wedged a hassock and a low chair against the screen, settled the backs of her hands on her hips, and quietly dared the result to fall down. The screen stood firm. She examined the remainder of the room, properly darkened for a restful night; the fire banked with ashes, her work; the roses on the windowsill, her work; chairs in place, tables cleaned, also hers. Hot milk in a vacuum jug on the bed table and the bottle of sleeping pills beside it. The milk was Hattie's work. But everything to hand in case it was needed. The milk and the pills weren't needed, not now. Sleeping like an angel, breathing nice and regular. When she was like that, Miss Sills didn't want her to have a pill. Miss

Sills had said she was the one to decide whether or not a pill was necessary and nobody but herself was to touch the bottle, either. She had said accidents could happen and sometimes did. "Not when I'm around," Emma had said coldly.

The mantel clock said nine-thirty. A good long wait before Miss Sills came back, Emma reflected, unless the rain drove her home early, which wasn't likely. Young people made out like they could walk between the drops.

She rubbed her eyes furtively. She was sleepy, and she longed for her own bed with its overabundance of thick quilts and the paper sack of hard white peppermints under the pillow. But she put them out of her mind, and her heart warmed with a martyr's glow. I'll wash my face with cold water, she told herself. That'll keep me awake. I'll just run down the hall to the lavatory—take me a couple of minutes, no more.

There was a bath adjoining the bedroom, but she obstinately chose to accept Miss Sills' instructions about that. Miss Sills said it was a private, not a public bath. Emma turned up her nose at the gleaming tile and spotless basins. Like a hospital. You could do an operation in it.

She gave a last, quick look at the figure on the bed. So flat, so thin, so still. Dark lashes smudged the pale cheeks; dark hair lay across the pillow. The old rug was spread over the eiderdown— she'd wanted it that way, you could tell. It was too hot, but Miss Sills could take it away later. And that massage, it was a punishing treatment. Those poor thin arms and legs, you'd think they'd break in two.

EMMA went quietly down the hall, stopping once to peer over the stair railing. The lower hall was dim. Her sharp old ears identified and placed the faint sound of music under the hardier sound of rain and vines blowing against the landing window. They were playing the radio down there, in Mr. Ralph's little study at the far end of the hall. Turned down low and the door shut. The masseur's report must have been good; otherwise, they wouldn't be playing the radio. If the report had been bad, they'd be glooming in and out of her room, keeping her awake with their talk about how well she looked and how she'd be horseback riding in another month. Not fooling a cat, either. Laughing and smiling all over. That's how they acted when the report was bad. A child would catch on .... And I'm no child, she added, even though they think so. I can read them like a book. That goes for Breitman, too, and I'll tell him the same the next time I see him.

She sent an indulgent smile down the dim stairs and pattered softly to the lavatory at the end of the hall. The afternoon towels hadn't been changed. Her job, and she'd forgotten it. Well, considering the company and all the extra work, you'd think Miss Sills would be kind enough to—Someone had left a tube of toothpaste on the washbasin. Miss Sills! Her brand and the top not screwed back on.

She studied the tube for almost a minute, then squeezed it in the middle and twisted it awry. That'll show her what cooperation is, she gloated. But when she admired her work, she felt uneasy. The result was so clearly a piece of thoughtful malice that she tried to straighten out the tube. But it broke and covered her hands with paste. She hid it in the towel hamper. The wastebasket was too public.

After that she was wide-awake and decided she didn't need cold water on her face. She started back.

Across from the lavatory a closed door stood in a deep recess. Every day she looked at that door and said a prayer under her breath. Now she looked at it again, and her eyes filled. The hall light lay softly on the smooth, waxed panels; but no amount of waxing and rubbing had been able to erase the old deep dents at the bottom or the new scars that bit into the area around the lock. That lock was new, too. It was so new that it glittered like gold.

The deep dents were made long ago by small, stout shoes kicking for admittance to an attic that was always locked a week before Christmas and kept that way until late on Christmas Eve. But no matter how careful they were, little Robbie managed to be around when the bulky packages were carried up the back stairs and smuggled through the attic door. No matter how quiet they tried to be, he always heard them and came on the run. As far back as the first rocking-horse time, when he couldn't run without falling down. The rocking-horse time was the first; then the scooter, then the tricycle, then the bicycle and the sled, not to mention all the other things, like railroads and trucks that cost too much and were big enough to ride in. Well, maybe they did spoil him. What happened later must have been their fault. A child grew up to be what you let him be. Yet—

She raised her eyes to the lock. The scars were deep. Once again she saw frenzied hands working against time with whatever tools they'd been able to find in the cellar chest. Once again she heard the heavy breathing of men doing something they never had done before, heard the hopeless clatter of a screw driver as it slipped through sweating fingers, heard the loud, insistent ringing of the front doorbell. Above it all, the ringing of the bell.... How long ago? Six weeks ago. Yes, six weeks.

EMMA turned from the door and went back to the room, walking slowly, with bent head. She was more than sleepy now; she was old and beaten, and she knew it. If she woke up dead in the morning, she wouldn't care. As she found her way to a chair by the banked fire, she told herself she wouldn't care at all. The light from the single lamp found and lingered on the rose-colored jug and the bottle of pills that stood on the bed table. Before she closed her eyes, she sent a long, compassionate look across the room to the figure lying under the blankets and rug. It was still. Of course it was still. But something that could have been a shadow rippled over the rug at the fold where the hidden hands lay. It could have been the shadow of the ivy that swayed in the wind outside the glass door. She told herself it was the ivy and the lamplight, and that satisfied her.

Emma went to sleep with her hands folded under her neat black apron, sitting upright in her chair. Sometimes she stirred in her sleep, because she was running away from a horror. She was running up the attic stairs, followed by bells and voices. And all the while she knew she was running in the wrong direction, but she couldn't turn back.

SHE heard Emma moan in her sleep like a tired and laboring animal, and the sound dragged her up from the depths of a beautiful dream. She was dreaming that her fingers had wrapped themselves around the fringe at last, had turned and twisted and grown strong. She fought to keep the dream, clinging in her sleep to the heavy strands, because they made a chain that bound her to life. No dream had ever held the ecstasy of this one. She could almost feel pain. She could almost persuade herself that her hands—

It was no use. She was awake. That was wishful thinking, she told herself despairingly; that was childish. She couldn't afford to be childish.

She opened her eyes and looked at Emma. Emma sat in shadow, the fireplace was dark, the corners of the room were darker. She couldn't see the clock, but Emma's presence and the screen, the jug, and the sleeping medicine told her it was still too early for Miss Sills. The screen, with its flanking chair and hassock, was Emma's work. Miss Sills could make it stand without support.

And there were four pills left in the bottle. It was easy to count them, four pills neatly covering the bottom. That was correct. She knew how many there ought to be; every night she counted them. The dose was one, and it was placed in her mouth and followed by a drink of the hot milk. When she couldn't see the bottle, or when the number of visible pills was uncertain, she refused the milk. There were too many opportunities for slipping extra pills into the jug. Sometimes the jug was brought by one person, sometimes by another, all the way from the kitchen, with stops en route to talk or answer the telephone. And sometimes there were as many as six people in her room at one time, all talking and moving about. And too often she was in her chair by the window, turned away from the table.

Four pills; that was right for tonight. Unless a new prescription had come and—Stop that. Stop. Don't waste emotion on imagination. Save the emotion for the things you know. Let the things you know feed you and make you strong. Listen to the rain on the roof, on the porch. Faint and clear and clean and measured. Like fingers on the keys of a typewriter in a distant room with a closed door. See how everything falls into place when you make your mind behave? Always make your mind remember the things it must. Try again. Begin again with the rain.

The rain has nothing to do with us, but it seems to belong. Perhaps because it sounds the way the typewriter keys used to sound. Night after night, before that day.

It didn't rain that day. That was the day of sun and St. Patrick's, and McCutcheon's and Tiffany's and the Plaza ....

She didn't go home when she left the Plaza; she shopped for another hour and then drove to the bank. Maybe Robbie would drive home with her, maybe Ralph, maybe even Bruce. There was no earthly reason Bruce couldn't drive out for dinner at least, and she'd tell him so. It was about time he paid them a little attention. A good dinner and a good talk. She'd ask his advice about Robbie. And she'd tell him he could leave early for whatever it was that kept him so close to town. Probably a girl, and a young one at that. He always looked foolish when she asked him what he did in the evenings. A very, very young girl, with plucked eyebrows. Men like Brucie are invariably trapped in the end by girls young enough to be their daughters.

When the car stopped at the bank, she had her own trap set for Bruce. She'd tell him how much she missed the long walks and rides they used to take together. She'd tell him he was almost as dear to her as his own brother had been. No. No, that wouldn't do. That might sound as if—She felt the color surge to her cheeks. Hussy, she said to herself, what a mind you've got.

She entered the bank and walked briskly to the offices in the rear. I'll simply tell Bruce that I'm worried about Robbie, she decided, that Robbie looks like the devil. Maybe he's noticed it himself. I'll remind him that he's Robbie's only relative and that, while Ralph does his best, it still isn't quite enough. And we'll have something very special for dinner, just the four of us, me and my three men. I'll make it a gala. I'll wear my new dress and that crazy rouge I haven't dared try yet.

SHE was beaming when she went into Ralph's office. Ralph wasn't there.

Miss Harper, his secretary, was doing her nails and looked embarrassed. "Mr. Manson left about an hour ago," Miss Harper said, "Can I do anything for you, Mrs. Manson?"

"No." She hesitated. "Do you know where he went? Home or the club or what?"

"He didn't say, Mrs. Manson, but I think he went home. He filled his brief-case, and when he does that—"

"Yes, I know." Ralph and his homework. Ridiculous, but he got a big kick out of being an executive, even after hours. Nice old Ralph, doing his best to act like a Cory and a banker and doing it too hard. "What about my son? Do you think the bank will bust if I take him home with me? I've got the car."

"Mr. Robbie didn't come back after lunch," Miss Harper said. "I believe he—I heard Mr. Manson and Mr. Cory mention it." Miss Harper's embarrassment had turned into something stronger. She didn't seem to know where to look.

"Mention it in what way? You mean they needed Mr. Robbie and couldn't locate him? They knew he was with me."

"Oh, I don't know anything about it, Mrs. Manson! Nobody said—I mean, I simply heard Mr. Cory ask where Mr. Robbie was, and Mr. Manson seemed to think he—I really don't know anything about it, Mrs. Manson."

She told herself Miss Harper was an idiot, a maladjusted, fluttering, stammering little fool. "It's all right, Miss Harper, thank you." She wanted to say that Robbie could come and go as he liked in his own father's and grandfather's bank. "I'll go in and see Mr. Cory. Perhaps he'll ride home with me."

Miss Harper started to say something about Bruce, discarded the sentence before it was fairly launched, and substituted a noisy and frantic hunt through her desk. "My bag and gloves," she explained, waving them as if they were a last-minute reprieve. "I know you'll excuse me, Mrs. Manson, but I've got to rush, I really have. Heavy date, you know, heavy date." She smiled falsely and scurried out of the office.

She followed Miss Harper slowly, aware of a sudden and unaccountable depression. Perhaps the gloves and bag *were* a reprieve. Miss Harper's pale eyes had shown an absurd relief when she held them up.

Bruce's office door was closed, and when she got no answer to her knock, she went in. Empty. All at once she was too tired to question even herself. She nodded to a clerk, who stopped at the open door with a startled look, and then she went back to the car.

All the way home she told herself she had been too happy in the morning. When that happened, you always ate dust in the afternoon. For no good reason, for no reason at all. Of course there was no reason. She planned dinner all over again, confident that all three would be home when she got there. All three, even Brucie. Brucie, coming out with the others for a surprise. But why, after all these months, why a surprise? Was it a silly anniversary or something? Had she forgotten one of her big-little days? No, she hadn't forgotten.

ON THE station side of the little park she saw Alice Perry walking with her head down. Alice looked dejected, not brisk and trim as usual. Poor Alice. Always too ambitious, always expecting too much of her two Georges, husband and son, never satisfied with the small, pleasant comforts of her life.

She raised her hand to beckon, then remembered something Ralph had said. She hadn't agreed with him then, but she dropped her hand now. He'd said: "Go easy on the indiscriminate lifts, darling. In bad weather it's all right, but you stop for anybody and everybody, and it looks patronizing. Especially to people like Alice Perry. She's apt to think you're rubbing her nose in your fine car."

She'd been indignant. "I've known Alice Perry since George and Robbie were children. I like her, and you're crazy, darling."

"All right, I'm crazy. But Alice doesn't like you. She wants what you have."

She'd laughed. Maybe Alice did want what she had, but that was only because Alice was born discontented. It wasn't a personal thing. They'd always been friends of a sort, as two women are when their children play together. Now she turned from the plodding figure and pretended not to see it. I don't feel like talking to her anyway, she told herself. I don't feel like talking to anybody. I want to get home in a hurry.

Emma let her in. Emma was wearing her hat, she'd been to the stores, and just got back. No, she didn't know if Mr. Ralph or Mr. Robbie had come home. She didn't know anything about Mr. Brucie. She'd look in the coat closet and find out in a minute.

"Don't bother," she told Emma. "I've got something for you to do. I'm going to call Mr. Bruce in town and ask him out for dinner. A very special dinner, because I feel that way. I want you to huddle with Hattie. Open all that stuff you've been hoarding, stuff like caviar, use all the eggs and cream and butter in the house, and get more. See if that man has pheasants. And don't tell me anything about it. I want to be surprised."

She went to her room and, still wearing her outdoor clothing and dialing with gloved fingers, called Bruce's apartment on her own phone. Why am I acting as if this were a life-and-death performance? she wondered. But Bruce's apartment didn't answer. She tried his club. He was expected for bridge, and she left word that he was to call her as soon as he came in.

The upper hall was quiet; the doors were all closed. They weren't home. When they were home, you could hear them through walls and doors. She drew her bath and laid out the new dress. Diamonds? No. Plain gold? Chic. Or sapphires? Yes, sapphires because her eyes—Hussy.

She was in the bath when she heard someone come into her room. "Ralph?" she called.

"It's Bruce, dear. I'll wait here until you come out."

"How perfectly wonderful! You're a mind reader! I've been trying to get you. You've got to stay for dinner."

"That's what I came for. Take your time, Nora."

"What's the matter with your voice? Got a cold?"

"No. I don't know. Yes, I guess I have."

"I'll fix that. I know the very thing. Is Ralph with you, or Robbie?"

"No. I came alone."

"Brucie, I went to the bank today. Am I screaming too loud? Anyway, I went to the bank after lunch with Robbie. I'm worried about Robbie, he looks awful. But you'd all gone. That crazy Miss Harper—I don't see how Ralph stands her ..... See Robbie anywhere around?"

"I haven't looked. How are you anyway, Nora? It's been so long—"

"Your fault." She left the tub and got into her dressing gown. "Be with you in a minute. If you want a drink, ring for Emma. This is going to be a party."

She went into the room and saw him bending over the laid fire. He was putting a match to the paper, and when he turned to greet her, his face was stiff and white.

"You really are sick!" She ran across the room and touched his cheek. "You are, and I love it. We'll keep you here tonight and take care of you. Brucie, if you want to marry a little fool, go right ahead. She'll be better for you than that creeping, crawling gentleman's gentleman. That man doesn't know the first thing about—"

Bruce was looking over her shoulder, and she turned. Ralph was coming in. Ralph didn't speak; he didn't have to.

They can't both be sick, she told herself. Not both of them, not all of them. Something's happened. They've got bad news, and they're here to tell me. The bank—No, Robbie! I knew it. I've known it all day.... She wrapped the dressing gown close; she was bitterly cold with a sweeping, numbing cold that rushed from all sides. She found a chair by the crackling fire and sat erect. "All right," she said. "Don't waste time. Let me have it. He's run away, hasn't he? He can't be dead."

"Dead?" Ralph's voice was startled, his face accusing. "Whatever makes you think— Bruce, will you?"

"Yes," Bruce said. "Nora, you haven't seen Robbie since you two had lunch?"

"You know I haven't!"

"Did he say anything to you—about us, about the bank?"

"No, no. But he looked dreadful. Go on, Bruce!"

Then he told her. Ralph stood by the window with his back to the room. As Bruce spoke, she knew it was right that he should be the one to tell her. Bruce and Robbie had the same blood.

He told her that almost two hundred thousand dollars had been stolen from the bank over a period of two years, a job so carefully contrived that no one had known about it until yesterday. There was no doubt about Robbie. She barely heard the damaging phrases, words like "estate" and "trustee"; she heard only that there was no doubt about Robbie. The Board was convinced.

Bruce and Ralph had asked the Board for a few days' grace. They were going to talk to Robbie—that was why they were both there. But Robbie hadn't come back from lunch, and that had forced their hands and frightened them a little. They had both looked for him.

"He wasn't at any of his old hangouts," Bruce said. "So I came here, because I was pretty sure he'd turn up, if only to see you. I don't think he's made a bolt."

"I don't believe it," she said.

"I find it hard to believe myself. But it looks—Apparently it began when he first came to the bank. We're going to give him every chance."

"He didn't do it."

"I want to believe that, too. We'll soon know, Nora. He'll tell us; he's no liar."

"He didn't do it. He wouldn't know how. Find him—both of you go and find him. How long have you been in the house, and what have you done?"

Bruce said he had come alone on the three-o'clock train, let himself in with the key he always had had, and seen no one. Then he'd gone for a walk and just returned.

Ralph said he had come on the following train, found Robbie's room empty and no one about, and locked himself in his own room to think. Ralph's hands, on the back of a chair, were white around the knuckles.

"Ring for Emma," she said.

EMMA came. She had a menu in her hand and began to read it aloud the minute she crossed the threshold. "Turtle soup," she said. "I don't care whether you want to be surprised or not, you've got to listen. A good turtle soup with sherry, not too heavy for what comes after and nice for a coolish evening. Then a small fresh salmon—" She stopped. "What are they saying to you, Miss Nora? What's happening here?"

"Have you seen Robbie?"

"I told you before, I haven't seen a soul until now. I was out from lunch on. But if you want to know if he's home, I guess he is. Or was. Hattie says she heard the typewriter going a while back. Up in the attic."

Bruce said quickly, "Attic?"

"Where else? That's where he keeps his machine, that's where he does his writing, the young monkey. Sometimes, when he comes home early, he just slips in and goes up there."

Ralph said: "I'll check. I'll go right away. That'll be all, Emma."

Emma stood where she was. "It will not be all," she said. "It's my right to know what's happening here."

They stood in a tight little group before the attic door and watched Ralph put his hand on the knob. The door was locked.

"He's taken the key," he said over his shoulder. He sounded as if he were swallowing a scream.

"Scream," she cried, "scream, get help. Scream, scream, or I will. Get that door open!"

Bruce ran downstairs. He was gone for a lifetime, in which Robbie was conceived, born, bathed and fed, sung to in the evening dusk, played with in the morning sun. She leaned against the wall and bore him again with pain.

Bruce returned with the cellar tool chest. The front doorbell rang and rang through the house.

"I'll pay, I'll pay," she heard herself say. "Restitution, recompense, I don't know the word. He didn't do it, but I'll pay."

"Stop that," Bruce said. "Somebody go down and send that woman away. Mrs. Perry. She's at the door. Somebody send her away."

Something heavy and metallic slipped through his fingers and clattered to the floor. She went down on her knees before the locked door. They were all on their knees, even Emma, pounding with tools, boring, prying, calling his name.

SHE knew her lips were shaping his name now. She tried to tighten them. Useless. She tried again. Better. Now she had her lower lip between her teeth, holding it fast. The muscles in her face were rigid, under control.

Could I do that yesterday? she wondered. Could I have done that a few days ago? Am I getting stronger or am I dreaming again? Don't dream; don't. You'll know when the time comes. Concentrate on facts, on things that have body and substance. If you don't, you'll lose your mind. Concentrate on anything. The bed, the lamp, the jug, the glass bottle. Never take the medicine unless you are able to count the pills. Remember that. Never take it unless you can count, and take it only from Miss Sills. If you could talk, what would you say first? If you could walk, which way would you go? No, no, think of something that is real.

This room is real; it has body and substance. The jug of milk, the bottle, the painted screen, all real. There are gray clouds and black birds and green rushes on the screen. That's right, that's right. And there's one small bird deep in the rushes at the bottom, sitting on a nest. Find the small bird on the nest. Low on the left, near the floor—you know where it is. Find it . . . .

There was a gloved hand lying on the floor under the screen.

It moved along the floor, in the space beneath the frame, a bright-yellow hand with thick, spread fingers. Another hand crept out and moved beside it. They minced to the right and then to the left, feeling their way, like two blind, glutted things.

Her lips curled back from her teeth.

The two hands traveled to the end of the screen and stopped. A few inches above them another hand crept around the frame and curled and slipped and clung. Then another. Four thick, yellow hands close together, beckoning....

"I don't know why you want to leave before your time's up," Mrs. Sills said to her daughter. "It's not half past ten yet. What do you think I cut that cake for? Not for myself, I can assure you. Stale bakery cake is good enough for me. I made that cake for my only child, who brings me a bundle of messy old uniforms and says it's such a bad night that she'd better be going out in it. Going where?"

Milly was unimpressed. "Don't give me that cake routine again. You're fifteen pounds overweight from four-layer chocolate fresh out of the oven. And I'll take my laundry to the Steam Hand, if you don't like it. I hate rain, and you know it, and George has a toothache."

"I begin to see the light," Mrs. Sills said. "George has a toothache, and Mrs. Perry won't let him out. So you haven't any place to go except to see your old mother. When I was your age, I had four or five on the string and glad enough to come running when I called the tune.... Are you going to marry him, or am I being personal?"

Milly said nothing.

"Don't do it," her mother said, "unless you can afford a place of your own. Don't do it unless he can support you. None of this career-after-marriage business, because when the babies begin to come and you have to stop work, they always get mad—because they miss the extra money and won't admit it. And don't economize on cheap furniture; it doesn't pay in the end. No veneers —good solid walnut or cherry. I'll give you half of my silver.... Was that George you called up a while ago?"

"Yes."

"I couldn't hear, because you lowered your voice. I don't know what you have to tell a man that your own mother can't know about."

"You couldn't hear because I didn't say anything. He wasn't home—or wouldn't answer the phone."

"Toothache!"

"Good-night, Mother." Milly started for the door.

"Have I said something wrong?" Mrs. Sills wondered wistfully.

"Not a word." Milly gave her mother a kiss and a hug. "I'm going to stop at Marge's to return a library book. Then I'm going straight back to my nice, sick baby, and I don't want any other kind for a long while. Now you know, and I'll drop in tomorrow afternoon on my exercise. If I can. Be good." She closed the front door and went down the short path to the sidewalk.

THE rain fell steadily, evenly, meeting the pavement with a hiss but sinking into the sodden grass without a sound.

You'd think it had a home under the grass, she thought. You'd think it had a special place to go. Worms. Nothing under grass but worms. But under this particular grass, under this very super Mrs. Nathaniel-Sills-and-daughter grass, there are also bones. Cat, dog, canary, and goldfish bones, in shoeboxes and matchboxes, all rotted and gone. I have the soul of a poet . . . . After that it was too easy to think of another kind of grass, trim and parklike, where the same rain was sinking into the earth and finding—

She ran past the lighted drugstore on the corner, turned and ran the length of a block to Marge Foster's shop. "Hi," she said in a breathless voice that she tried to make casual.

Marge, sorting rental cards at her worktable, looked up. "Put that umbrella in the stand before I drown. What brings you out in all weathers?"

Milly slid her book across the table. "I make it twenty-four cents due. Here's a quarter, and I want change."

"You kill me," Marge said. "I can remember the day when you patronized Carnegie's Free. Why don't you go back there? Sit down. How are you, honey?"

"So-so." Milly pulled up a chair. Miss Foster's Lending Library and Gift Bazaar was empty except for the proprietress and Milly. "Terrible night. George is sick. He says. Mother's going to give me half her silver. She says. What do you know, Marge?"

"What do *I* know? You're the one who lives the life."

"I'm gaining weight—they feed me swell. On some cases you share a bowl with the dog."

"You're lucky. You look wonderful." Marge gave the rain-blurred windows a rapid survey. "I don't feel like business, I feel like talking to an old school tie. Put your feet up and relax." She crossed to the door, locked it, and returned. "And they call me money-mad."

MILLY settled her feet on the edge of a bookshelf. "I ought not to stay, honestly. I'm not due back till twelve, but she's acting kind of funny tonight. Got a cigarette?"

"Here." Marge pushed the box across the table. "Milly, you know I'm as safe as houses. I wouldn't open my mouth about anything you told me."

"I haven't got anything to tell. Match? Thanks. What's the matter with you? You look as if you didn't believe me."

"Sure I believe you. George Perry's mother was in this afternoon, looking for 'a little love story, nothing modern.' The whole time she was here she was talking at the top of her lungs about how her son is the light of Mrs. Manson's life. Is he?"

"Of course not. Half the time he's there she doesn't even look at him. If I know you, Mrs. P. said something else and you're working up to it. What?"

"Well, she did want to know how well I knew you. Casual-like. Quote: 'Are you very friendly with that little nurse of Mrs. Manson's? I believe Mrs. Manson has become quite attached to her.' I don't think she loves you."

"She doesn't even know me. I'm taking my time about that. What else?"

"She thinks Bruce Cory is too good-looking. She sort of hinted that he liked Mrs. Manson too well before she up and married his brother. To say nothing of marrying Manson, too. And now that he's hanging around again, using her illness as an excuse—Her and her little love stories! Milly, is Mrs. Manson going to die?"

"Not if I can help it." Milly turned and looked at the dripping windows. They showed a strange, new world. But the single, wavering blur of light was only a street lamp that stood on the curb; the twisted shape that rapped on the pane and sprung away and rapped again was nothing but a branch. "Not if I can help it," she repeated. "I'm a good nurse. I know that. And Babcock must think so, too, or he wouldn't have wanted me. Not for a patient like Mrs. Manson." Milly's voice grew soft. "She's a darling, she's a pet, and I worry about her all the time. I want her to get well. I want her to get even half-well. The minute she shows a definite improvement, they want to take her away somewhere, a change of scene. Any kind of change ought to help. But I don't know. The other day I dressed her up in her jewelry, rings, bracelets, clips—stuff to knock your eyes out. But she no like, I could tell. Had to take it all off and lock it away. Emma says it was on her dressing table, ready to put on, the day Robbie died. Maybe that's why she doesn't like it."

"I like the way you say 'died.' All right, but you don't have to look at me like that. Is Emma nice to you? In books, the servants are terrible to nurses."

"She's okay. She isn't like a servant; she sort of runs things. She's been there years and years. Emma was the one who found her."

"I KNOW." Marge removed her glasses and polished them thoroughly. "Change of subject coming up. Somebody was in here yesterday asking about you."

"Who?"

"I don't know. A woman. She looked sort of familiar, but I couldn't place her. This shop is like a railway station. Strangers drop in maybe once or twice a year, motorists and so on, people from New York buying a book for a weekend present. Maybe she was somebody like that, just a face I'd seen once before. Anyway, she didn't know you, didn't know your name. She wanted to know if I was acquainted with the nurse at Mr. Manson's."

"Maybe somebody who used to know them. Didn't like to inquire at the house. You know, tragedy and all that."

"Maybe. They came from New York themselves years ago. But I got the idea it was you she was interested in."

"Me? No. You know everybody I know. Funny. What did she say?"

"Nothing much. She just ambled around, bought a couple of Halloween cards, and acted friendly in a pushing way. You know, the great big smile that goes with spending ten cents. First she asked how Mrs. Manson was getting along—lots of people ask me that, because they know I know you or they've seen you in here. Then she wanted to know where you lived."

"For heaven's sake! I'm getting a reputation."

"Think so? Wait. She said, 'Does the young lady live in Larchville, or did they get her from New York?' I said Larchville. And I also said what do you want to know for, but in a nice way, of course. And she said she thought maybe she knew you and was just making sure. She did a lot of smiling and hemming and hawing and said she thought maybe you'd trained at the hospital with her cousin or somebody. She said she was interested in young nurses starting out who'd trained where her cousin had."

"Crazy. No sense to it. Who's her cousin?"

"She very carefully didn't say, even when I asked." Marge lighted a cigarette. "Know what I think? I think she was a snooper, a busybody, one of those women who try to get the dope on other people's troubles so they can brag to the bridge club. She had a face like bridge-every-afternoon; sharp. Also heavy around the hips, too many of those bridge desserts. So when she said your name had slipped her mind and wasn't it Johnson or something like that, I closed up like a clam."

"Right. Thanks."

Marge was thoughtful. "You know, there could be something behind it, Milly. Something like family trouble, for instance. She might be a relative of the Cory family, still sore about Manson's marrying the money Cory left. Or she might be an old girl friend of Cory's—I mean the first husband."

"Did she look like the kind of girl friend a Cory would have? They say Bruce is the living image of his brother. Was she the kind of woman a man like Bruce Cory would—look at?"

"From what I've seen of him I'd say no, but fast. Her clothes weren't any better than mine. She was all right, you understand, but she didn't have the kind of manner you expect in a woman connected with a Cory or a Manson. But you can't always tell about boys like Cory and Manson."

"What a brain," Millie admired. "Sensational!" She dragged her feet from the shelf. "After eleven. I ought to start back."

"Aw, wait. I've got coffee. It's on the hot plate."

With the coffee they had bakery doughnuts, which tasted better than four-layer chocolate because they came out of a paper bag.

It was ten minutes to twelve when Marge locked the shop door behind them. They walked to the corner before they separated. Marge stood on the curbstone and watched Milly cross the deserted street and strike out in the direction of the park. The slight, raincoated figure and the big umbrella were swallowed in mist and fog. The rain had turned into an aimless drizzle.

Marge went home and tried to remember where she'd seen the woman who was interested in young nurses. The woman was beginning to fill her mind .... Not a one-shot customer, Marge decided. I'm sure of that. Maybe somebody who just moved to Larchville, one of those people you stand next to at the grocery store. Maybe. Green coat and hat. Drop a brick out any window this year, and you'll hit that same green coat and hat.

MILLY let herself in. One light was burning in the hall, the one they always left burning when she was out. It was a signal for her to put the chain on the door. It meant everyone else was in. She fixed the chain, turned out the light, and crept upstairs.

The doors along the upper hall were closed. All except Mrs. Manson's at the front. Light came from that doorway, a dim, straight shaft on the dark hall carpet, like a path cut through shadows. She stopped in the lavatory and brushed her teeth with just water, because she couldn't find her toothpaste. Her hooded coat and umbrella were dripping, so she hung them on the lavatory door.

Emma was asleep in a chair before the dead fire, but she'd done her usual job on the glass door and screen. Milly grinned at the screen, anchored with chair and hassock. One of these nights Emma would use the bureau, too.

She walked to the bed. Mrs. Manson was awake, wide awake. Her face was white, and her eyes were glittering. "Hey," Milly said softly, "what's the idea?" She remembered then that the door to the hall was open and went back to close it. We're about to have a little one-sided argument, she told herself, but we needn't let the whole house in on it. "Hey," she said again, "you're bad tonight. What makes you so bad, honey—I mean, Mrs. Manson?"

Mrs. Manson's eyes met hers.

"Now, wait," Milly said. "One thing at a time. You don't like something, I can see that. Well, we'll take care of it, we'll toss it right out, whatever it is. But the pulse comes first." She drew the cold hands from under the rug and held one limp wrist.

The eyes clouded; then the glitter returned. They gleamed like the eyes of an animal caught in a trap that was imperfectly sprung. Milly had seen a squirrel once—

The pulse was too rapid. She held the cold hands in hers. "You're frightened," she said. "I know. But it's all over now. Milly's here. Still, I don't know why your hands should be freezing, you've got plenty of blankets and the room's exactly right. Nervous about something? Now, now, you mustn't be." She sat on the edge of the bed and talked softly and persuasively. "I bet I know what happened," she said. "You had a bad dream. And because you're sick and sort of helpless, you couldn't throw it off. Now me, when I have a bad dream, I practically kick myself out of bed and wake up screaming. They're terrible, aren't they? But everybody has them once in a while, pal—I mean, Mrs. Manson. I mean, you're not the only one."

No, that wasn't it. According to Mrs. Manson's eyes, it wasn't a dream. They said so, as plain as words. They said they had seen something.

Milly felt a prickle along her spine. Got me doing it now, she thought. Not that I haven't been getting ready for it. Bones in boxes.... For two cents I wouldn't look over my shoulder, even at Emma.

She rubbed the hands gently. They were like ice, but Mrs. Manson's forehead was beaded with perspiration. Get busy, Milly told herself. Get to the bottom of this, but don't let her see that you're worried. She couldn't possibly have seen anything. There's nothing to see. Maybe she heard—

"LISTEN, honey, I'm going to wake Emma up and send her to bed. And maybe Emma can tell me what—what you want." She went to Emma and touched the old woman's shoulder. Emma was a heavy sleeper. Milly had to shake her awake.

"Well," Emma said. "Is it time for you already? I must have dozed off."

"You must have taken one of Mrs. Manson's pills. What happened in here while I was out?"

"Nothing." Emma was indignant. "You don't have to glare at me like that, Miss Sills. Everything was as quiet as you please. We slept like a baby, same as if you'd been here." Emma looked at the bed. "She's all right. Even I can see that."

"You're as blind as a bat," Milly whispered. "She's anything but all right. No, Emma, don't go over there now. I want to talk to you."

Emma struggled to her feet, blustering and protesting. "I'm sure I don't know what you're getting at, Miss Sills! I can see as well as you can, and I say she's all right."

Milly said: "Please keep your voice down, Emma. Who was in this room tonight?"

"Nobody. What do you think I am? I wouldn't let anybody in. Mr. Manson and Mr. Cory stopped for a minute or two before the masseur came, but you know that as well as I do. And that's all."

Milly observed to herself that the whole town of Larchville could have trooped in and out while Emma was having her doze. Aloud she said: "Did Breitman say anything while he was here? Did he say anything about her condition?"

"Not a word. He never does. He's very close-mouthed. He and I talked the same as we always do, nothing more. Miss Sills, I—" Emma began to break. Milly's stern young face was full of foreboding. "Miss Sills," she wavered, "if anything's gone wrong, while I—Miss Sills, what's gone wrong?"

"Mrs. Manson is frightened, and I want to know why. At first I thought she'd had a nightmare, but now I'm not so sure. I think she may have overheard something. Or she may have been— remembering things again. That's always a bad business when you're alone at night, to say nothing of being sick.... Exactly what did Breitman say?"

"Nothing. Nothing about her. He never spoke her name once. We talked about the weather. He said the country was nice after New York, and he liked to come out here. That's all."

"Didn't say anything that she could misunderstand? Mention any names, any names at all?"

"No, Miss Sills. Just the ordinary talk, like we always have. She wasn't frightened then, Miss Sills, I know it. Because after he left, I washed her face and hands and covered her up good, and she was nice and drowsy. I was thinking maybe she wouldn't need her pill tonight and how that was a good sign." Emma's hands were limp against the folds of her black apron, but her voice said she was wringing them mentally. "I'd like to stay here tonight," she beseeched. "I could sleep in a chair. If she's going to have trouble, then this is where I belong."

Milly softened. "No. You get your regular sleep. But I promise to call you if I need anything."

"Mr. Manson?"

"I'll call him, too, but not now. The fewer people in here the better. Run along, Emma. Say good-night to her, but make it snappy and happy."

Emma hesitated. "You know that second bell on the wall over there rings in my room, don't you? My own room, not the kitchen. It rings right over my bed, nice and loud. If you should—"

"I will." She eased Emma to the bed and watched the old hands gather up the younger ones and fold them under the rug.

When Emma looked down at the face on the pillow, she obviously didn't trust her voice. But she covered the staring eyes with one of her hands, gently, as if she were telling a wakeful child it was time to sleep.

MILLY closed the door behind Emma and went back to the bed. The room seemed darker with Emma gone, darker and quieter. Even larger. I'm crazy, Milly told herself. A fine state of mind I'm getting into. Missing Emma, thinking of Emma like the Marines. This is what they told us in training. This is what they said would happen sometime, and I thought they were bats. They said there'd come a time in the night, in the wards and in homes, when you were on duty alone and felt as if you were being watched. Not by a patient, by something else. They said it was a natural thing and not to be frightened. That's what they said. But some of the older nurses, the old war horses who'd seen everything, they said it was death watching you. Waiting for you to turn your back .... She turned around slowly, looking into every corner of the room and listening. What she saw was luxury and security, what she heard was silence. She bent over the bed. "Never let the patient know you're nervous," they said. That's what they said.

She smiled. "Time for the nightcap," she said, "and maybe I'll join you." She took the bottle of pills and reached for the jug of hot milk. "I'll get the bathroom glass for myself. I can use some of this milk. I'm worn thin; we had too much company today." She smiled steadily. "You probably feel worse than I do—you can't tell people to shut up, and I can."

She knew Mrs. Manson was watching her hands as they uncorked the jug and filled the cup. She replaced the jug and shook a single pill into the palm of her hand, talking all the while. "If the sun comes out tomorrow, I'm going to park you on the sleeping porch. Tomorrow's Sunday, you remember that, and old George will be home all day. Maybe he'll hang out his window with his face all tied up like the Robber Kitten. He says he has a toothache. Well, we'll make fun of him and he won't know it .... Here you are. Open wide."

Mrs. Manson refused. It was more than mutiny; she tightened her lips in a straight, hard line, and her eyes blazed. The muscles in her throat were like cords.

Milly stared, holding the milk in a hand that shook. Her eyes widened with delight. Mrs. Manson's throat muscles were the most beautiful things she had ever seen. They were strong, pulsing, and controlled. For the first time.

She exulted. "Well, what do you know about that! You ought to see yourself! You're still a bad girl, and don't think I'm not mad at you, because I am, but I do believe you've turned the corner!

You hear that? You're better! You couldn't make those mean, ugly faces a week ago. You couldn't even make them this morning. Well, am I tickled!"

But there was no responsive smile, and that was what she wanted most of all. Response. Anything that would prove cooperation and receptiveness and settle the question of a clouded mind.

"Mrs. Manson, smile. Smile just once, and we'll forget about the nightcap."

The agony in the eyes that returned her look was almost more than she could bear. Mrs. Manson was trying to smile, but she might as well have tried to run.

MILLY said: "Never mind, never mind, baby. Forget it."

She rolled the pill about in the palm of her hand; it was a capsule, and it rolled lightly and evenly. What am I going to do now? I can't force her—not when she looks like that. But I've got to make her understand that I'm on her side, that the things I ask her to do are the right things. I've got to find out why she's terrified. She can't go through the night this way. Neither can I. If I try the milk again, if I try selling myself with the milk—

Aloud, she said: "Mrs. Manson, please take the milk. I won't bother you about the pill. I know you hate it even though it's good for you. But please take the milk. This is my job, Mrs. Manson, I need it. Doctor Babcock might send me away if he found out that I couldn't—couldn't persuade you. And I don't want to go away. Please, Mrs. Manson, just a little milk for my sake."

Mrs. Manson's eyes filled with tears. They gathered slowly and clung to her lashes. Only when there were too many did they begin to fall.

Milly put the milk back on the table and dropped the pill into the bottle. "I want to help you," she said miserably, "but I'm helpless myself. I can't think of anything to do. Can't you give me a sign of some sort? Can't you look at something in the room that will give me a clue?"

Mrs. Manson's eyes blazed with hope. It was a look that even a child could have read.

"There, now," Milly rejoiced. "You see? We're all right, we're fine. We're getting this thing licked, aren't we? Is it something in the room that frightens you, something I don't know about?"

The eyes met hers and held, like a hand reaching out to take another hand. They directed her to the bed table. There was nothing on the table but the milk jug, the cup of cooling milk, and the small glass bottle. And two linen handkerchiefs, neatly folded. The same things that were there every night.

It couldn't be the handkerchiefs. They were her own, marked with her initials, N. M., in a little circle of flowers. There was nothing frightening about a handkerchief. She shook them out. They were clean, empty, fragrant. She touched one of the wet cheeks and studied the table again, following the direction of the eyes, pinning the look to a definite place. The pills?

"Now, you're not afraid of those pills, Mrs. Manson. You've had them every single night. They're the same as always; we haven't changed them." She turned the bottle between her fingers. "See? Same druggist and everything. Same old stuff. Four little pills for four more nights .... Well, I'll be! I've hit it, haven't I?"

The look had changed; it was eager, urgent, full of horror. It was almost like speech. It warned and pleaded and prayed. Mrs. Manson had been in the depths, she was still there, but she was emerging.

AFRAID of the medicine all of a sudden, Milly marveled. I'll fix that right now. She got her handbag and put the bottle in it, holding the bag so Mrs. Manson could see every move. "See?" she said. "Just as good as thrown out. And tomorrow I'll tell Babcock you like it the same as you like poison." Poison. That crack about poison when they were all having drinks in the afternoon; that might have started it. Lying alone, half-asleep, half-awake, listening to the rain, thinking back. When she returned to the bed, she said: "Those pills are okay, silly. I'm just humoring you because I think you're nice. All right now?"

No, Mrs. Manson wasn't all right. She still looked at the table; her eyes still talked. Her lips, stiff and dry, struggled with the shape of a word. Mrs. Manson was seeing something that only she could see, and she was trying to tell about it. It was hopeless, and she knew it, but she was trying.

Suddenly Milly was engulfed and defeated. This was hysteria, this was something she couldn't fight alone. Manson? Cory? She looked at the bedroom door, at the glass door. George? Beyond the glass door and the porch, across the garden, George was safe in his own house. She went to the screen and walked around it, unconscious of the horrified eyes that followed her. It was cold on the porch, and the wind was wet and mournful. It sighed in the trees and the ivy, and touched her face with damp fingers.

George's room was dark, the whole cottage was dark. She looked to her left, along the length of sleeping porch. The porch ran to the end of the house, wide and shadowed, overhung with trees and vines. Mr. Manson's room opened on it, so did Bruce Cory's. But their rooms were dark, too. There were no lights showing in any of the rooms that she could see.

Mrs. Manson must have been all right when they went to bed, she thought, or they wouldn't have gone. They'd have waited for her or called Babcock. Then she knew what she wanted to do. Call Babcock. It was only a quarter of one. He wouldn't mind, he was used to late calls. And it was later than this the night he came to her house and asked her to take the case. He was crazy about Mrs. Manson.

She went back to the room, smiling easily. "I'm going downstairs to get you a drink of water. Ice water. You won't mind if I leave you for such a little while." She didn't wait for an answering look in Mrs. Manson's eyes. She wanted to get away, to hear Doctor Babcock's reassuring voice, to hear his booming laugh. He'd tell her that hallucinations were common in cases like Mrs. Manson's; he'd say he'd be right over.

SHE closed the door quietly and went down to the first floor, hugging the stair rail, not turning on lights. She didn't want to wake the others. Not unless it was necessary. At the rear of the hall she fumbled for the kitchen door. There was no sound anywhere. And I used to have ideas about Bruce Cory, she scoffed. I had the repartee all ready. He doesn't even know I'm alive.

When she was safe inside, she closed the door behind her and found the light switch. The kitchen phone looked beautiful in the clear, strong light.

Doctor Babcock's housekeeper answered after a long wait. Milly knew the woman slightly, but she didn't identify herself. "Doctor Babcock, please."

"He's not here."

Her heart sank. "Do you know where he is? It's fairly important."

"No, I don't know. He got a call around ten, and he hasn't come back. You want to leave a message?"

"No. No, thanks. I—Did he say how long he'd be?"

"He said he didn't know. He said he might be a long time, and I was to lock up. I wouldn't be surprised if it was a confinement."

"Oh. Well, I guess—well, if he comes in during the next hour or so—" She thought of Babcock ringing the bell, rousing the house, Emma, Hattie, Mr. Manson, Bruce Cory. She saw Emma and Hattie peering from behind doors, Mr. Manson and Bruce Cory, bathrobed and tousled, stumbling down the stairs. She began to have doubts. They might think she'd been forward, calling the doctor without consulting them. And suppose, after all that, they went to Mrs. Manson's room and found her asleep.

Asleep in spite of herself, exhausted by her own imagination. That happened sometimes. They'd think *she* was the crazy one.

"Well?" The woman's voice was impatient. "Are you still there, and if you are, what do you want me to do?"

"Oh, I'm sorry. No, there's nothing, thank you. I'll see Doctor Babcock in the morning." She hung up. She could call again. In another hour, if Mrs. Manson was still awake. She filled a glass with water from the refrigerator bottle and went back the way she had come.

SHE watched the door, waiting for Miss Sills to return. Miss Sills was taking more time than she needed for a glass of water, and that was good. It was good if it meant that Miss Sills had stopped in the kitchen to make cocoa for herself. Sometimes she did that. If she did that tonight, if she drank cocoa that she herself had made, then she wouldn't be thirsty, then she wouldn't drink the milk in the jug. Sometimes she drank what was left of the milk in the jug. Everybody knew that. Miss Sills told everybody about it and laughed. If she drank the milk tonight—

When the hands had come, she had tried to scream. She screamed silently in her heart and soul while Emma slept by the fire. She watched the dark, shapeless mass that crept from behind the screen and cavorted on the floor, dragging its thick, yellow hands. Hands where feet should be. It was big enough to stand alone, strong enough, but it didn't stand. It rose and fell like a strong black jelly and made a sound like laughing. Then it went away.

The clock on the mantel ticked on. Minutes passed, uncounted. She watched the screen.

Then the door to her room opened quietly, and she turned her eyes in an agony of hope. *Emma, Emma. Try to hear me, Emma.*

She watched the silent approach over the soft rugs, the deft opening of two capsules, the addition of their contents to the jug of milk. The refilling of the capsules with her talcum powder, the refitting of the halves, the return to the bottle. She was ignored as if she didn't exist. She might not have been there. She was the same as dead then ....

"Here you are," Milly said. "Did you think I'd run away?" She held the glass of water to Mrs. Manson's lips. "Right out of the icebox. Now, you and I are going to sleep whether we feel like it or not. I'll leave the light on. And I won't go to bed. I'll do my sleeping in a chair, right where I can see you and you can see me. Now, don't look at me like that. It's all right. I've done it lots of times before, and you never knew it."

She moved Emma's chair to the bed; any chair that Emma selected for herself would be comfortable. Mrs. Manson watched. The eiderdown from the cot, an extra blanket for her shoulders.

The chair faced the bed; it was nearer the foot than the head. Its back was to the screen.

Before Milly settled down to what she told herself was a sleepless night, she opened both sides of the porch door. George's room was still dark. She sent him a wan smile across the garden and returned to the chair. It wasn't too bad; it was almost as good as a bed.

Then she got up again.

She knew there was another cupful of milk in the jug, and she was thirsty. She filled the empty water glass with the milk and saluted Mrs. Manson before she drank.

Miss Sills was nodding. Soon Miss Sills would be asleep. A deep sleep. In the morning Miss Sills would have a headache.

In the morning I will be dead ....

How will it happen? It couldn't have been planned for tonight—no one could have known she'd drink the rest of the milk. It was a lucky break. The way had been prepared for a lucky break, and it had come. And it wasn't needed, it wasn't necessary at all. It was simply an extra precaution, a weapon in reserve, devious, typical.

How long will I have to wait now?

Not long. This is too good to miss. It would have been better if there'd been more time for frightening me. It must have been a wrench to give that up. I see the whole thing now, I know the plan. I was to be frightened out of my wits until that grew tiresome and wasn't exciting any more. Then, when the time was right, when I was alone or with Emma only, I was to be killed. How? Perhaps smothered. Smothering will be easy.

Emma left me alone tonight. There was plenty of time then. Emma was asleep tonight, over by the fire, out of sight of the screen. There was time then, too. But I had to be frightened first, because that was exciting. That would have gone on night after night until it got to be a bore. Or until a foolproof opportunity came. An opportunity too good to miss. Like tonight.

WERE Miss Sills and I being watched? Yes, of course we were. But what difference does that make now?

Soon the hands will come back and move along the edge of the screen. The black shape will rise from the floor and stand up, and one of the hands will uncover the face, and I will see it.

The face is being saved for the end, like a big scene. Like a scene at the end of a melodrama, when the audience is supposed to be surprised. It won't be played for my benefit; the face knows that I know now. It will be played for the excitement the actor gets.

I know even about the hands. I know what they are. Moving along the floor, under the screen, close together as if they belonged to an animal.

That is too vile.

Miss Sills is asleep. Her head is bowed. She sleeps like a little girl.

When they find me in the morning, will they say I turned in my sleep and smothered myself? "She turned in her sleep—the pillow. It's the miracle we've been waiting for, but we didn't know, we didn't think—"

Will the police believe that?

Miss Sills sleeps like a little girl.

Can they do anything to her? Can they accuse her of negligence? Or will someone suggest that she was in love with—

Waiting is dreadful. Why is it taking so long? ...

At last .... Miss Sills. Miss Sills. *Miss Sills!*

PART TWO

I T WAS Hattie who screamed. The sound ripped through the quiet house, rose and fell, and left in its wake a deeper silence than before. It dragged Emma from the refuge of sleep.

Emma's room was separated from Hattie's by the bath they shared. She knew where the scream came from, but the hush that followed it was endless and shocking. She told herself that everybody was dead. There was no breath in the house; when people are sleeping and breathing in a house, you always know it. She sat up in bed and turned on the light. She wanted to see the clock although she was convinced she had no more need of time.

It was three o'clock. She covered her mouth with a thin, gnarled hand, to keep herself from screaming, too. Then she heard other sounds, doors opening and closing, feet on the floors above and on the stairs. Feet on the kitchen floor, a chair overturned. Voices. Someone knocked on the door to the kitchen. "Emma?" It was Mr. Cory.

She managed to say, "Yes, sir?"

"We want you out here."

She opened the door. "Mrs. Manson, Miss Nora—"

"We want you in the library," he said.

She put on her robe and slippers and pinned up her scant braids, taking her time because the next few minutes would tell her something she didn't want to hear. When she reached the library, Hattie was already there, alive, and wrapped in a blanket.

She looked for the others—Mr. Cory, Mr. Manson, Miss Sills. Mr. Cory was standing by the fireplace, Mr. Manson was telephoning, Miss Sills was absent.

"Miss Nora?" Emma faltered. "Miss Sills?"

"Miss Sills is all right. Everybody's all right except Mrs. Manson."

"Not—"

"We're trying to get Doctor Babcock. Mrs. Manson is unconscious, and Miss Sills quite rightly refuses to accept the responsibility. We don't know what—Emma, can you do anything with Hattie? Nothing she says makes sense."

Emma turned on Hattie. Hattie's shrill, wailing voice rose above the telephone conversation, but they heard enough of the latter to know that Doctor Babcock wasn't home.

SHE hadn't slept well, Hattie said; the ivy had kept her awake. All night long it had been making noises at her window, scratching against the wooden shutters, and she'd listened to it for hours before she'd made up her mind that she couldn't stand it another minute. She'd got out of bed then, not turning on a light, and found the scissors in her workbasket.

"I was going to cut it off," she said. "The ivy. I could see it moving back and forth, a long, black, ugly-looking thing out there in the dark. Like a snake. So I was going to cut it off. And then—" She stopped short when Manson left the phone.

"I got hold of Pleydell," Manson said. "He's younger than I like, but he's the best I could do. Get on with it, Hattie."

"Yes, sir. So I was going to cut it off. I was half out the window and had it in my hand when the arm came down."

Cory looked at Manson. Their faces were white, but they smiled and shrugged. "There's no reason you should listen to this again," Cory said to Manson. "Why don't you wait at the door for Pleydell? He hasn't far to come. Emma and I—"

Manson left gratefully.

Emma said: "I don't want to hear the rest of it. She's crazy. I want to go upstairs. I want to see Miss Nora."

"No," Cory said. "We've got to kill this thing right now. Your window is only a few feet from Hattie's. You may be able to persuade Hattie that she—"

"Nobody's going to persuade me, now or ever!" Hattie wailed. "And not Emma Vinup either! I tell you I saw an arm, a long arm, six feet long if it was an inch. It could've choked me to death and would've done it, too, only I frightened it away!"

"Away where?" Cory's voice was soft.

"Don't ask me. Away, that's all. I think up."

"Up where?"

"How do I know?" Hattie thought it over. "If it went down, it would've gone down to join its body. And I'd've seen a body if there was one, because it would've been standing on the ground right in front of me. There wasn't a body. There was only this arm, hanging down like the ivy, right in front of my face. Six feet long if it was an inch, with a yellow glove on."

"Yellow! Hattie, listen. It was dark, it was—"

"A yellow glove, Mr. Cory. There's some light out there, you get a little light from the street lamp. I saw that glove like I see you. It swung sideways, like it was looking for something to hold onto, and it hit me in the face." Hattie touched her cheek with a fat finger, and her eyes rolled. "Not hard, but I felt it. Like it didn't know I was there."

Cory turned to Emma. "Doesn't that sound like some kid warming up for Halloween?"

"Not," said Emma, "at three in the morning. This is a nice, residential district. It was something she ate. Go back to bed, Hattie. I'll come in and see you later." The look she gave Cory said that she was in control and he was less than nothing.

WHEN Hattie had gone, trailing her blanket and sniffling, Emma made sure the door was closed. Then she said: "Mr. Brucie, what happened upstairs? What happened to Miss Nora? Was it Hattie screaming like that?"

"It must have been."

"But could she hear it? Her door's always closed at night. I've heard Hattie many times before. She did break her record tonight, but that's a long way off. I don't know, I—"

"The porch door was open," he reminded her. "And Hattie's window is on that side of the house. I think we can assume it was Hattie's work."

"Unconscious." Emma was thoughtful. "I never knew her even to faint. Never. Even when Robbie—you know that as well as I do! She never was the kind to faint and carry on."

"But she's sick now, Emma."

"Are you telling me? And there's something else, too." Emma frowned. "She was upset tonight, what you might call wild-eyed. Miss Sills thought she'd had a nightmare." She told him about Miss Sills' return at midnight. "Miss Sills was sharp with me, too, as if I'd done something. Me! I'd lay down my life, and you know it. Miss Sills said Miss Nora was terrified, that's what she said."

Cory walked to one of the long windows. "Lights on over at Perry's.... How terrified? When a woman can't speak, can't move—"

"It was the way she looked. She looked awful." Emma faltered. "It could have been a bad dream—but it wouldn't go away when she woke up. She couldn't shake it off. Miss Sills sent me down to my room. She said she could handle it better alone. I don't know what she did, though."

"That was midnight?"

"Yes. Twelve or a little after. Mr. Brucie, what does Miss Sills say?"

"Miss Sills seems to know less than anyone else. She didn't hear Hattie. She didn't know anything was wrong until I woke her up. She wasn't easy to wake, either. And Nora—" He prowled about the room.

Emma fought for patience. "If it's a cigarette you're looking for, then for mercy's sake, sit down and let me get it." She found matches and cigarettes in a table drawer. "Here. You heard Hattie yourself, didn't you?"

"Of course. My door was open and the back stairs—I went to Mrs. Manson's room at once."

"I'd have thought you'd have gone to the place where the scream came from."

"You'd have thought nothing of the sort. You'd have done as I did.... What are you listening to?"

"Somebody came in the front door without ringing the bell. Can that be the doctor so soon?" She opened the library door. Voices came down the hall. "George Perry, wouldn't you know it, and the new doctor, too. He looks too young. I'm going upstairs. I can be useful." She was gone before he could stop her.

GEORGE wore a raincoat over his pajamas and galoshes on what he said were bare feet. He breathed as if he had been running. "I saw your lights go on," he said to Cory. "I was looking out my window. If you're going to search the grounds, I can help. That's what I came for."

"Do you know what you're talking about?" Cory asked mildly.

George said: "I think I'd better sit down. I'm winded. Sure I know. If you're trying to keep this thing a secret, you're out of luck. I met Pleydell on the porch, and he told me, but I didn't need that. I got an eyeful myself, and I'm not surprised that Mrs. Manson passed out."

Cory studied George closely. "Exactly what do you think you saw?"

George colored. "I don't know," he admitted. "Listen. I'm far from being the kind of guy who hangs out windows spying on the neighbors, but—"

He told Cory he'd gone to his window to spit out a dental poultice, and he looked ridiculously young when he said it. "I looked across the grounds to this house because—well, there it was and there I was, and I saw something moving. Back and forth, under the porch. I thought it was a dog, a big dog, maybe a collie. But there aren't any big dogs around here. So I kept on looking." He said the dog prowled close to the house, as if it were stalking something, and that was all right, because the place was full of moles and so on. Then it disappeared. By that time he was wide-awake and he went to get a cigarette. When he returned to the window, the dog was on the sleeping porch. "No wonder Mrs. Manson fainted, big brute like that, strolling around the porch, walking in her room, place half-dark."

"Do you have a theory about how a dog could climb that porch?"

"The tone of voice is all right with me," George said agreeably. "I didn't see him go up, but I saw him come down. He came down like a monkey. Maybe he was a monkey. I saw him swing over the railing and hang on the vines. Come to think of it, I didn't actually see him hit the ground. By that time I was falling around my own room, looking for my shoes. Maybe he was a monkey or maybe he was the Hound of the Baskervilles. I don't know or care, much, except that he ought to be found and shot. He gave me the creeps.... How's Miss Sills?"

"There's nothing wrong with Miss Sills."

"I'm glad to hear that." George's voice was faintly chiding, and he looked as if he had more to say, all of it censorable. But when he continued, he was mild enough. "And how come Pleydell instead of Babcock? Not that I don't think Pleydell is good. I do. My mother had him once, and he saw through her like a window. But I thought Babcock had this house staked."

"Babcock's out on a case."

"Pleydell says Hattie woke the dead."

"Yes. Now see here, George, don't talk about this to anyone but me. You'll have us in the papers, and there's been enough of that. To say nothing of demoralizing the neighborhood. You know our Hattie."

"I sure do. I used to help Hattie set traps for nonexistent mice. This time, according to Pleydell, she saw an arm six feet long."

"Pleydell talks too much. So, apparently, does Manson."

"So, and I'm not kidding, will my mother. Wait till she hears this one! I slid a note under her door, telling her where I'd gone. In case you wanted me to stick around for a while and help search. You know, in case we decide to take it seriously."

"Now, George—"

"In case we found something that looked like paw marks. The ground is soaking, so they'd show. Or something like torn leaves, broken twigs, and so on. Or footprints. It could have been a cat burglar, you know. Man instead of dog; object, Mrs. Manson's jewelry."

"All insured."

"But not enough to pay for being frightened out of your wits. I'd feel better if you and I slipped outside and took a look around. We could take a quick look and satisfy ourselves."

Cory was indulgent. "Stop romancing, George. I'm satisfied now."

"I'm not," George complained. "Some of the porch ivy is hanging loose, and it wasn't like that this afternoon. I saw it just now by Hattie's window."

"It's too dark to see anything like that, and you know it."

George put his hand in his pocket. "Not with this," he said. He played his flashlight around the room. "I used it when I came across the garden. I saw what I saw, all right."

"Put it away, George, and grow up."

"That's what my mother always says," George agreed. "Grow up. Oh, well."

They sat on without talking. The doorbell rang once, and Cory answered it. When he came back, he said it was Babcock.

Babcock had finally returned to his house and found the message Manson had left.

George ambled about the room. He showed a mild interest when Pleydell, young, red in the face, and clearly unrecovered from a snub, came to the door and asked to be taken to Hattie. Cory led him away. After that, George's wanderings took him to the garden windows. He whistled softly. His father and mother, armed with flashlights, were picking their way across the wet grass, turning into the path that led to the front door. His father was only half-dressed, but his mother was gloved, hatted, and veiled. He went back to his chair and waited for the bell to ring.

MILLY said she didn't need anything. Mr. Manson said: "Yes, you do. Come downstairs for a drink when you're through in here." Then he left to answer the doorbell.

Milly stood by the bed with Emma and Doctor Babcock, touching the smooth covers to reassure herself, talking softly, although there was no need for that now. Mrs. Manson was mercifully asleep.

Babcock listened, one plump hand embracing his chin. When she finished her story, he said: "Absurd. And dreadful."

"I didn't hear a thing," Milly said. "It wouldn't have frightened me if I had. I've heard Hattie give out before—she does it when she thinks she sees a bug. But poor Mrs. Manson—"

"There, there," Babcock said. "It's all over now."

Milly looked at Mrs. Manson's closed eyes. Pleydell had been wonderful. He brought her out of the faint, or whatever it was, and talked as if he gave her credit for being adult and sensible. He described what he called Hattie's nightmare as if he'd dreamed it himself, and he made Emma laugh with him. Mrs. Manson listened, her eyes never leaving his young face. Then he gave her a sedative, but not from the bottle on the table. His hand went toward the bottle, but her look stopped it in midair. So he took a bottle from his very new bag and held it for her to see. Even then she refused; she looked at Emma as if she were talking to her. And Emma said: "I'll sleep here, I'll sleep in the same bed. And it won't be the first time, either." After that it was all right; now Mrs. Manson was asleep, and Emma was sitting on the bed and yawning and all but telling them to get out.

Babcock touched Milly's arm. "Come, Miss Sills, there's nothing more for you to do here. You heard what Mr. Manson said. A small refresher—you've earned it, and I need it. A long, trying day, a miserable night." He led her from the room and guided her along the hall as if she were ill.

She was relieved, she'd been afraid he'd blame her for sleeping. He was being fair and understanding. Two wonderful men, Pleydell and Babcock. She was lucky.

ALL the doors along the hall except two were open; there were lights in the rooms. On the right, the rose guestroom adjoining Mrs. Manson's bath—the room Mr. Manson used now. Rose blankets thrown back, rose sheets dragging on the floor, the porch door open and the curtains not drawn. Mr. Manson had left that room in a hurry. A funny-looking room for Mr. Manson to be sleeping in.

Robbie's room on the left. That one was locked. It was always locked. It would be dark and dusty if you could see inside. Were the sheets still on Robbie's bed? Plain white sheets, wrinkled where his body had lain; soft white pillows showing the print of his head? No. No, that bed would be smooth, because he hadn't slept in it.

Beyond Robbie's, the room Bruce Cory used. A brown room, an English-looking room, like those you saw in English movies. Plain dark furniture, heavy and handsome; brushes and jars on the big chest, tortoise, ebony, and crystal. Expensive. Mr. Bruce Cory got out of bed like a Boy Scout, no matter who screamed. No matter what. Sheets folded back, dark-brown blankets neat and tidy. The lavatory next door. Then the stairs that went down to the kitchen.

Across the hall from Bruce Cory's, Mr. Manson's suite that he wasn't using. But someone had been in there. Lights in the bath and in the dressing room. Drawers pulled out of the dressing-room chest. As if somebody wanted something in a hurry. Handkerchiefs on the floor, a dark-blue scarf trailing from an open drawer. Everything dark blue and cream.... Wanted what in a hurry? A revolver in the handkerchief drawer? That could be. A scream in the night....

The second closed door was next to Mr. Manson's suite. The attic door. Doctor Babcock's hand pressed her arm. "My arm must be shaking," she decided. "My knees are. And my head aches." She smiled at Doctor Babcock, to let him know she was grateful. The wide stairs to the first floor were straight ahead.

"Take things easy tomorrow," Babcock said. "Don't worry about your patient, she's in good shape. Take long walks, think of pleasant things. We can't have *you* cracking up!" They went down.

She had seen George's father before, puttering in his flower beds, a graying, gangling replica of George. His old tweed topcoat, worn over pajamas, was wet and wrinkled. He looked cold and unhappy as he huddled by the fire. Alice Perry was a familiar figure, too, and also from a distance. Alice Perry was complete, from pearls to corset. No one introduced them.

Milly went to a chair by a window, out of the circle of light. Cory brought her a drink. When she had time to look around, she saw Pleydell in a far corner, making himself small in a huge chair, looking like a choirboy waiting for words from a bishop.

It was after four o'clock; it could have been four in the afternoon except for the dark windows, the lamps, and the assorted clothing. George looked like a perfect fool. She'd tell him so when she got the chance. And he was grinning. There was nothing to grin about.

ALICE PERRY was laughing, a brisk, efficient, party laugh. "Ordinarily I sleep like a baby," she declared, "but tonight I was restless. Of course, I heard George prowling, but I thought it was his poor tooth. Then I heard my big George, also prowling. Such men! That was when I got up and found little George's amazing note. Of course we came at once—the neighborly thing to do. Dear Mrs. Manson. I'd cut Hattie's wages if she were mine."

Everyone laughed.

"The villain was the wind," Cory said. "George says the ivy's down. Of course that's what she saw."

"Oh, naturally, the wind," Alice Perry agreed. "Our poor chrysanthemums, absolutely beaten to the ground. I showed you, dear, as we came over. George dear, *big* Georgie, didn't I show you?"

Mr. Perry nodded.

"The wind was pretty stiff," Manson said. "Frightful racket in those old trees, almost human. So human that for a minute I thought Hattie was a particularly big blow."

Everyone laughed again. Hattie is a very comic character, Milly thought. All you have to do is mention Hattie's name, and everybody howls.

Babcock took it up. "The wind was bad in town, too. I didn't like it at all."

"The wind, the wind," George chanted. They all looked at him. He was playing with his flashlight, turning it on and off.

"Put that thing away," Alice Perry said. "It looks silly, and your hands aren't clean."

"The wind, the wind," George said again. "I am forcibly reminded of a little blue-and-gold copy of *A Child's Garden of Verses*. Robbie and I each had one; we learned some of the stuff by heart; we were very, very cute. I quote. Title: *The Wind*. Line:

'And all around I heard you pass—like ladies' skirts across the grass.' Did it sound like that to any of you, or am I just being sentimental?"

They laughed at George almost as much as they'd laughed at Hattie. Even little Pleydell made a cooperative sound, but he kept it up too long.

Milly looked at him with sudden anger, and he colored. Why do I always get interested in fools? she asked herself. Why am I down here, anyway? Why doesn't George introduce me to his parents? Why do I stay, like a dope? Because I am a dope. She got up. "Excuse me, everyone," she said. "I belong upstairs."

They began to talk again before she left the room. She heard Babcock say something about the masseur. His report had been a good one. Babcock had called him in town. They were going to try the treatment every night. Mrs. Manson was responding. George said something about Hattie and the masseur.

Milly closed the door on a fresh burst of laughter. George had started them off again. He had an I.Q. of six.

She was halfway up the stairs when George came after her. He didn't say anything, but he put his arms around her and held her close. It was better than putting a ring on her finger. It was the first time he'd ever done that. His I.Q. rose to the height of heaven; exactly heaven.

"Be over in the morning," he whispered.

That light is the sun. The Sunday-morning sun. That is Emma over there. Emma, coming out of the bathroom with the vacuum jug, the cup, the glass. All clean, dry, sparkling; everything washed away. No traces left. Nothing.

Watch Emma through your lashes. The old trick.

Emma is rubbing the damp places on the carpet, blotting out the prints of four hands. She is brushing dried leaves from the floor and talking about the wind. Soon nothing will be left of the night. She is destroying me.

There is a crack in the bowl of the lamp. Will she see that? A new crack in my fine lamp. She won't like it, she'll be angry, she'll talk about it. Emma or Miss Sills, either will do. Emma or Miss Sills, bending over the bed, saying: "What a shame. Something happened to her lamp, and she liked it so much. Does anybody know what happened to her lamp?"

My lamp was knocked to the floor by two thick yellow hands in a hurry. And after that there was not enough light. Not enough to see in, not enough safely to kill in. No sound, except the thud ·of the lamp and the breathing of two people. Not my breathing. I held my breath in the dark, and it was the same as hiding. Two people breathing, Miss Sills in the chair and the other at the head of the bed. Slow, drugged breathing for Miss Sills; rapid, frightened breathing for the other.

She waited for Miss Sills to wake. Miss Sills hadn't heard the lamp go over, but she'd heard something. Or felt something. She'd stirred in her sleep and moaned. Poor Miss Sills. No, rich Miss Sills. Rich, powerful Miss Sills, who had given her the gift of another day.

The four hands had scrabbled over the floor to the screen and safety. Frightened off, but playing the part to the end. If Miss Sills had waked, she'd have seen a shapeless mass on all fours. She would have screamed as Hattie screamed. Then: "My dear Miss Sills, you are not yourself. It's been too much for you. A few weeks' rest—." Then there would be no more Miss Sills. Then there would be no more.

Will the lamp be taken away before someone sees the crack, someone who is all right? And if so, what excuse will be given? ... Never mind that, you know the lamp will go. Forget the lamp, try to remember the rest of it. There may be something, some small thing.

Hattie. How much later was that? One minute, two minutes? Who thinks of time in that kind of dark? The new doctor that Ralph called in was too young, too inexperienced, but kind and instinctively wise. He'd known at once that it was useless to offer the pills from her own bottle, but he didn't try to find out why. His bottle was a new one, and he'd let her see him open it. A safe, new bottle, and with Emma in the room all night as well as Miss Sills.... That's enough, that's enough, go back to Hattie. Maybe Hattie—

The new doctor said Hattie screamed because she had a nightmare. But Miss Sills said Hattie had been frightened by the ivy outside her window. They believed what they said; it was what they'd been told. But Hattie knew every leaf on that vine, every loop and tendril. What Hattie had seen was a black shape with four hands, but she would be talked out of it. If only Hattie would talk first, talk everywhere, to everybody. Even to tradesmen. Tradesmen gossip and pass things along. Had there been light enough for Hattie to see the hands? If Hattie talked about the hands, and it reached the right person—Who is the right person this time? Who knows about the hands?

Who knows? You do. You saw him making them. It was a secret, a joke. He told you he was making them for a present. He said, "Who's always asking for two pairs of hands?" He laughed when he said it.

Think, think. There was someone else who knew, someone who came into the room and saw. Who? Who came in? ... Now, now, you're doing it the wrong way again. You're letting your mind wander, you're seeing his face. That's bad for you. You're hearing his voice again. Stop for a minute and think of something else. Call yourself the nice names Miss Sills calls you. It isn't a foolish thing to do. Go on. Call yourself a good girl, a honey, a baby.... I'm a good girl, a honey, a baby.

Now go back to last night. Maybe you've overlooked something, something that will talk for you, point a finger for you. Soon. *Soon.*

The lamp that rolled to the floor. The darkness. The waiting. The scream. Then nothing. Nothing, nothing, nothing. Give up.

"You're awake," Emma said. "That's fine. And Miss Sills has brought your breakfast. You slept like an angel, and that's because you knew I was beside you."

Emma fed her, using a spoon and the glass tube, chirping and fluttering, full of importance. "Telephone ringing like mad—everybody heard about your fright and wants to say they were sorry. Only ten o'clock, and people come to call already. Doctor Babcock, the Perrys, and that nice little new doctor. But he went away again. Mrs. Perry brought a lovely jelly for your lunch and a bottle of sherry. Now eat this egg, and I'll let them all come in to see you."

Miss Sills arranged her chair. "Too cold for the porch," Miss Sills said. "I think we'll sit in the window. All cozy in the sunny window, and you can doze like a little cat. You need more sleep, you know…. Look, Emma, she wants that old rug. All right, you can have it when we get you settled. You're spoiled, that's what you are. Next week I'm going to use discipline."

Emma put the breakfast tray in the hall, and they wheeled her to the window. She heard the others coming, walking softly as befitted people who knew she had weathered a bad night.

"Let me see your feet, the lot of you," Emma said. "I saw you out in the garden, and I'll have no more things tracked in on my clean floor."

"Things?" George Perry.

"Leaves and grit all over. Tramping in and out of here last night, and I had to clean it up on my knees."

They surrounded her chair, smiling, paying their compliments. She was brave, she'd behaved like a soldier. She was a fine woman, getting better every day, no doubt about it. She was good-morning, Mrs. Manson; she was dear Mrs. Manson, who frightened them so. She was okay, Mrs. Manson, okay.... She closed her eyes, because she didn't want to see their faces. The voices told her where they stood and sat.

Miss Sills, on the window seat, spoke to someone. "No, don't take the rug away. I know it's hot, but she wants it."

"Is she asleep, Miss Sills?"

"Only relaxed. It's a good sign. She's always like this when you come in. Don't stop talking, go right ahead. She likes to hear voices around her, doesn't she, Doctor Babcock?"

"Oh, quite, quite. And what, may I ask, is the immediate future of the good neighbor's sherry?"

Ralph, doubtful, hesitating. "Well, I suppose we might—"

"It's eleven o'clock," Doctor Babcock said. "We had a hard night."

"You men! That's a *special bottle* for Mrs. Manson!"

"Emma, do you think—"

Emma, full of pleased complaints at the social turn of affairs, brought the house sherry from the dining room. The voices murmured on. Emma rattled glasses, rustled back and forth, and finally subsided. "I'm thankful to sit down. My legs ache. I'm an old woman, but nobody thinks of that. A person needs two pairs of hands around here."

Listen! Listen! All of you listen! Emma's quoting someone, Emma's teasing—can't you hear? Watch Emma's eyes, watch where Emma's looking. Say it again, Emma. Emma, say it again!

"Thank you," Emma said. "I don't care if I do. I'll get as giddy as all get out, but I like a nip now and then."

"You may have anything your heart desires, Emma. The house is yours."

"I'm glad to know that," Emma said, "because I want something this minute."

Then it came.

Emma said, "I want your permission to get rid of that lamp by the bed."

"What's wrong with it?"

"It's awkward, that's what. The shade's too big. It gets in the way."

Emma. Look at the lamp. Look at it.

Is Emma—no, wait, don't open your eyes. They're moving about; someone has come to stand behind your chair. Careful. Someone is waiting to see if you—*Take your hand away from my neck. Can't you wait for the dark?*

"Hey!" Miss Sills was beside her. "Hey, what goes on here? What have you got to shiver about? You're as warm as toast. Easy, honey, easy. All right now?"

"Lamp," George said. "That reminds me. Say, is it all right to talk about last night?"

"Why not?" Doctor Babcock. "Last night is already forgotten. Lamp, did you say?"

"Yeah. At what I figure was a crucial moment, somebody turned it out."

"What are you talking about?"

"The lamp Emma doesn't like. I was hanging out my window, and suddenly this room went dark. For about two or three minutes. The little one by the screen was already out. But the big one by the bed went out, stayed out, and came on again."

"You're crazy," Miss Sills said. "It was on when I went to sleep, and it was on when Mr. Cory woke me up. Wasn't it, Mr. Cory—or am I the crazy one?"

"Nobody's crazy, and George is right. The lamp was on the floor when I came in. I fell over it." His voice was rueful. "But I got it back on the table, and it worked, thank God. That was a bad minute."

"Floor?" George was puzzled.

"Floor?" Miss Sills repeated. "Well, I didn't hear it fall. I didn't hear a thing. I ought to be fired. All I know is that Mr. Cory nearly shook my teeth out trying to wake me up and Mr. Manson was running around in circles. Excuse me, Mr. Manson."

"My dear Miss Sills, that's libelous. I ran in a very straight line, in the wrong direction. Straight down the back stairs, because I'd recognized Hattie's clarion call. Then, halfway down, I heard Cory begging you to show signs of life at the top of his lungs."

Doctor Babcock was torn between grief and laughter, sighs and chuckles. "Dreadful, dreadful, but not without an amusing side."

"I didn't hear a thing," Miss Sills repeated. "I ought to be fired, but please don't."

"You ought to have more sherry." Bruce, walking to Miss Sills. "Here, all's well that ends well. And speaking of Hattie, have any of you good people ever heard a moose?"

They seized Hattie's name, hugged it and tossed it about. Hattie was a moose. She looks like a moose. The left profile? No, silly, the right! And isn't there a wart, too? On the nose? Stop, stop, I haven't laughed so much in years. Dear Mrs. Manson would love this, we must tell her when she's better. Hattie is a moose with a wart. Hattie—

Emma called from across the room. She sounded happy. "Look! Look here! This lamp's got a crack in it. It's not fit to use; it's not safe. This lamp's going to the White Elephant Sale at All Saints'." The cord and plug struck the carpet softly.

"Emma, how perfectly wonderful!" Mrs. Perry said. "Mr. Manson, do let us have it. I'm chairman this year, and it's simply dreadful the way people won't give us things."

"I don't know, but I don't see why not."

"I can't tell you how grateful—George dear, will you carry—George, stop whistling. Not nice, when poor Mrs. Manson—George!"

George said: "All right. But how do you suppose a heavy lamp like that managed to fall over? Could that be the wind again?"

"Wind? Oh, undoubtedly. She couldn't do it herself, poor lamb."

"Blowing leaves and little sticks, not to mention grit and mud. My nice clean floor. We'll have to keep that porch door shut," Emma said.

"By all means keep it shut," George said.

"George, what are you mumbling about?" Alice Perry asked.

"I'm quoting poetry to myself. My little blue-and-gold book."

"Well, stop it. No one's interested."

"I am. Listen. Still the pretty one about the wind that rips the ivy off the porch and blows a fifteen-pound lamp around. 'I saw the different things you did, but always you yourself you hid.' ... I think we ought to go home."

Chairs moved at once, quickly; glasses were set down on tables and mantel; voices mingled; sentences overlapped. Mr. Perry, you haven't said a word. George darling, no more sherry. The lamp, Mrs. Perry, don't run off without your white elephant! Lovely, lovely, and all for foreign missions, it means so much. George, I said no more sherry, it gives your eyes a funny look. Thank you for calling, thank you. Yes, we're on our way, Miss Sills. Don't look so pleased, we're all going. These little sherry parties are good for all of us. George? George, I'm not going to speak to you again.

GONE. Everything gone.

Emma collecting the glasses. Emma washes everything, the fingermarks, the muddy prints. Emma gave the lamp away. Nothing left, nothing, and the prints on the floor were clear, even I could see what they were .... Emma saw the crack in the lamp, and they said it was the wind.

All but George! There was something in his voice, wasn't there, wasn't there? He knows there was no wind, not enough for that, doesn't he? George, remember the wind; you made a joke of it, but you know it isn't a joke, don't you? Keep remembering the wind, remember the little book with the poems in it. I gave you that book, George. I gave one to you and one to Robbie. Robbie and George, George and Robbie. They were always together.... George!

George is the one who knows about the hands, George saw them when I did, George is the one I was trying to think of! George is the right person, the safe person!

Emma knows the phrase about the hands, but that's all. Stop, go slowly, make a list like a shopping list. What do you need?

You need Hattie to have seen the hands; you need Hattie to talk. You need George to hear. You need Emma to use the phrase again. You need George to hear. You need—you need George to remember.... But if Hattie—

That hand on my neck. I thought my heart would stop then.

Listen. Emma.

"You can carry these glasses down to the kitchen on your way out," Emma said to Miss Sills, "but don't you go waking her up to say good-bye. I'll sit right beside her all the time. She won't lack for anything if she wakes, and if she looks hungry, I'll see to her lunch. No need for you to hurry yourself. The doctor says you're to take it easy. And don't stop in the kitchen gossiping with Hattie. If you want the truth, that woman hasn't got all her buttons. That's a pretty coat. I always favored red. Get along now."

"Yes, Matron," Miss Sills said....

Miss Sills is going for a walk, wearing her red coat. Watch for Miss Sills. Open your eyes and watch for Miss Sills. No matter which way she goes, you can see the red coat. Look at the children in their Sunday clothes. Dark blue and brown for the big ones, pale blue and pink for the little ones. Nurses, parents. Young parents, full of pride. Who is that woman in the green coat and hat?

Emma, don't talk. Emma, be quiet! Emma, that woman in the green coat and hat!

"So you've decided to wake up and take notice, have you? I'll set my chair right here beside you. I know you —you were playing possum for the others, but the minute you knew you were alone with old Emma, you decided to wake up. That Miss Sills, there she goes, over to see her mother, I expect. Well, bless my soul, look at that rug! What happened to that, I want to know! I tucked it in myself, as tight as tight. You can't have—bless my soul, you're all tied up with fringe. A person'd almost think—but no, you can't do that…. There, that's better. That won't hurt my girl again. Such an ugly, big red mark…. Miss Nora, you aren't even listening to me. What are you looking at? What's out there? Same old thing that's there every day, unless it's Miss Sills. Of course, if you can't even listen to your old Emma…. Well, I hope you're satisfied. There she is, traipsing along like she didn't work for a living same as the rest of us!"

It is! It is! Miss Byrd. The nurse I had before Miss Sills. She wore that green coat when she went away! She came back! She came back, she had to come back. She knew something was wrong, she couldn't hide it, I could see her trying to hide it. She knew, or saw, or guessed; she watched everybody; she was uneasy. She showed it in the way she watched and listened. So she was sent away…. The patient is unhappy, Miss Byrd; we'll have to make a change. You understand that this is no reflection on your work. There's no criticism of you, Miss Byrd, none at all, but the patient isn't happy, and we can't have that. Mr. Manson thinks perhaps an extra check—we're very grateful…. She hadn't looked surprised; she'd almost smiled. She'd looked as if she'd expected it.

Miss Byrd. Everybody laughed at the Byrd because she looked like a hawk.

Miss Byrd, Miss Byrd, I'm up here in my window. Listen. That girl in the bright-red coat is my new nurse. Stop her, Miss Byrd, say something, anything. Make friends with her. Her name is Sills, Milly Sills. She's a nice child, she'll be courteous and kind. Talk to her—you'll know how to do it. Tell her what you know. What do you know, Miss Byrd? What did you see or hear? She's almost there, Miss Byrd, the girl in the bright-red coat and no hat. She's there, see, she's there! In front of you, in front! Say good-morning, say it's a lovely day, ask her the name of the park, ask anything. Stop her, Miss Byrd. *Miss Byrd!*

Now, now, close your eyes again. Don't cry.... You're a good girl, you're a honey, you're a baby. You're my good, good girl.

The lamp is gone; the tracks on the floor are gone. Miss Byrd—forget Miss Byrd. You have another day, this day. How much of this day do you have? Six hours? Six hours until dark. Spend them to the last minute, not on hope, not on fear. Spend them in preparation for tonight. Tonight you will be going—

This is the time to climb the attic stairs again. Climb the attic stairs the way you did before, and raise your head when you get to the top. The way you did before. That is a preparation of a kind.... Climb.

ALICE Perry circled her living room with the lamp in her hands, measuring the table tops with speculative eyes. "Nobody but Nora Manson would have cupids and a ruffled shade. At her age! For a young girl's room, yes; rather sweet for a young girl, but Nora Manson! Cupids!"

"That thing's Dresden," George said mildly. "Bruce Cory gave it to her last Christmas, and she bawled him out. It cost like the devil." He went to a window and looked across the hedge. "Emma's too openhanded with other people's property when other people can't talk.... Did you happen to see Cory's face while that was going on?"

She said: "I wasn't watching him then. George, this crack won't show when the lamp is properly placed. It might look rather fine against the right kind of wall. A soft, gray wall. You know, if I thought people wouldn't— George, don't you think it will be perfectly fair if I—"

"Sure," George said. "Give the White Elephant Sale a buck and tell the All Saints' ladies you took a piece of junk off their hands."

Alice sat down with the lamp in her lap and gave her son a bright smile. "Where's your father, dear?"

"Upstairs, lying down until lunch. I think I'll do the same."

Alice smiled again. "What's wrong with you, dear? Toothache, too much sherry, plain meanness, or are you in love with Nora Manson, too?"

"God help me," George said, "and I'm not swearing." He took the chair opposite his mother. "Say some more. Don't stop."

"Well, Bruce Cory's in love with her. I've always thought so, and I made up my mind to watch him this morning. Ralph Manson must be blind. Love, hate, sometimes you can't tell, but the way Bruce Cory looked at her! If Ralph Manson would come off his high horse and pay a little attention to his wife and her brother-in-law, he might see what I did."

"What did you see?"

"Well—oh, nothing. I simply mean—oh, you wouldn't understand."

"I might."

"No. You've always made a heroine of Nora Manson. I've often thought you cared more for her than you did for me. But I never interfered. I've always wanted you to have the best."

"This," George said, "gets crazier and crazier. I haven't been in that house a dozen times in the past year. At least, not until Robbie—"

"Now what have I said that's wrong?" Alice sighed. "Such a long face. Don't you like to talk to your own mother?"

"Robbie, I was thinking about Robbie. Sure I like to talk to you, but when Robbie's name popped up—"

"Morbid, dear."

"No. I have a conscience about Robbie. I didn't know he— Listen, there's something I've always wanted to ask you. Did you see Robbie that last day?"

"I? Certainly not."

"But you went there to call that afternoon for the first time in months. You got as far as the front door, and they stopped you. I've always wondered how you happened to choose that particular day and hour."

"I have an idiot child," Alice mourned. "I did *not* choose that particular day and hour, and I was *not* stopped. I simply had a feeling that I wanted to see Nora Manson, so I went over. But when I was told it was inconvenient, naturally I went away."

"Not far, though."

"Not—"

"I was coming down the street from the station when you left their porch. You walked around to the side of the house and looked up at the attic window."

ALICE flicked the ruffled shade with a careless finger. "Very well then, so I did. And the explanation is childish, so you ought to understand it. When they opened the door, I heard Nora Manson crying, and it worried me. Although we'd grown away from each other, I never once let myself forget that we both were mothers of sons."

"You didn't have a hunch about what was going on? You didn't see anything? That little trek to the attic window was unadulterated mother-for-mother instinct?"

"George dear, I don't expect you to understand my feelings. Wait until you have a child of your own. I hardly knew what I was doing. I don't even remember now."

"I can help you out there. You looked up at the attic window and then you got down on your knees and hunted in the grass. I was practically enchanted. Four-leaf clovers?"

She said, "Why haven't you mentioned this before?"

"It never came up before. That day, Robbie's day, is shrouded in a black cloud that seems to cover everybody. The way people act, you'd think the world stopped then and everybody stood still."

"All right, but don't look like that." Her eyes shifted from George to the garden window. "I did see him. Robbie. I was sitting in that window, and I saw him run up the path to the house. 'He's home early,' I thought. 'What a pity Nora isn't there.' I'd seen her drive off in the morning, all dressed up for town. Then after a while I went to my room to change for my little walk, and quite by accident I noticed that their attic window was open. Robbie, I thought, working at his writing when he ought to be out in the sun. And then the most extraordinary thing happened. I saw something fly out the attic window and fall in the grass. Something shiny. I was really agog. But I didn't do anything about it. I took my little walk, and then I felt like seeing Nora Manson. And I call this a silly conversation!"

"It was the key."

"What?"

"The key to the attic. Robbie locked himself in and tossed it out."

She didn't speak at once. Then: "You didn't see me pick it up."

"No. I saw you get up and go home. You're right about this conversation. Why are we having it? It's ancient history, dead and buried. Like Robbie. Who started it, anyway?"

She said, "You started it."

"Maybe I did. Well, nobody ever found that key. Manson had a new lock put on."

"I saw it this morning.... Here we sit as if I didn't have a thing to do. I ought to be getting lunch, and I don't feel like it. Look at my hands—disgusting! Dishwater! I don't know why other women can afford maids and I can't. There's no better manager in Larchville than I am, yet I never have a cent left over. Money! It makes me sick."

"Maybe you think too much about money."

"Well, if I do, it's because I'm the only one around here who thinks at all. Look at you and your father. Look at Ralph Manson. Look at this house and look at theirs. I knew Ralph Manson when he was nothing but a clerk in that bank, and now he practically owns it. All a man needs in this world is a little ambition to get ahead, a little common sense about the future, like—"

"Like what?"

"Like not falling in love with a penniless nobody, and you know what I mean.... If she dies, he'll be rich."

"No," he said easily, "if she dies, Cory will be richer. It's Cory money. And with Robbie gone, too—"

She fretted. "I really must do something about lunch. George, how rich is Bruce Cory?"

"Rolling."

"More than Ralph Manson?"

"Manson has a damn' big salary, and he's in with the money-making crowd. It all helps."

"That's what I thought.... George, what's out there, what are you looking at?"

He was at the garden window. "That's Milly's red coat. She's going for a walk. She doesn't usually go at this hour."

"You heard them pampering her, didn't you? Rest, drink this, eat that, take care of yourself, you're precious. Manson, Cory, and Babcock. Men!"

"What do you think of Milly, Mother?"

"I'll do my thinking about that when the time comes. George, are you sure you really—"

"I'm sure."

MILLY picked up the gold-and-scarlet ball that rolled between her feet and tossed it gently to the fat blue reefer with brass buttons. It came back at once, this time to her stomach. She returned it again. "You're an apple dumpling," she said, "but that'll be all today."

She had reached the far end of the park; there were no more benches, but across the street, where the buses stopped, the Larchville Women's Civic League had built a circular seat around the trunk of a spreading maple. Home was a few minutes away, with possible roast chicken and certain chocolate cake. And talk. But she wasn't hungry, and she didn't want talk. Not the kind she'd have to give, and take.

I won't be able to hide a thing, she told herself. I never can. Her mother would worry and say it wasn't safe. She'd try to make her leave the case. I won't go home, she decided.

Hattie was bats, pure bats. Washing the sherry glasses and rolling her eyes toward her bedroom. "You can go in and see for yourself, Miss Sills. That ivy's still hanging there, a fresh break in the vine. A long, thin piece like a snake, not like an arm. The arm was an arm, not ivy."

She'd listened to Hattie with amazement and disbelief. She'd said, "What's all this about an arm?"

Hattie had described, explained, and relived the night. The arm had a hand on the end of it, a six-foot arm and a yellow-looking hand. Or light-looking. A big hand, all spread out. A starfish-looking hand, like in the aquarium. "It came down and swung in front of my face, and then it went up."

"Up?"

"Up where it came from. I don't know where that was, but that's where it went. I wasn't asleep, Miss Sills, I wasn't dreaming. And what's more, I heard feet over my head. But nobody listens to me, not even the doctors. 'Don't let Mrs. Manson hear you talking like that, or we'll have to give you a bad-tasting tonic.' If I hadn't waked up when I did, we'd've been robbed."

"By a starfish hand, yellow-looking?"

"I hope you never have to laugh out of the other side of your mouth," Hattie had said.

Now Milly walked to the seat under the tree and sat down. When she thought of what her mother could do with Hattie's hand, she quailed. No, she couldn't face that. She'd rest a while and then go back. Nobody knew what Emma would do next. She might let the Perrys in again. That had been too much. Mrs. Manson had looked dreadful.... Mrs. Perry, saying, "So you're Miss Sills?" And turning away. Mr. Perry, patting her shoulder and saying nothing. George—

A voice beside her said, "You have a good heart."

A woman in a green coat and hat was smiling at her. "I hope you don't mind if I sit here, too. I was watching you in the park. You're nice with children—that's what I meant by a good heart."

Milly flushed. "Thank you."

The woman was familiar in an indeterminate way. Sharp, thin face, thickly powdered, and a spotted veil. The rouge and powder were like a mask.

"You're Mrs. Manson's nurse, aren't you?"

"Yes, I am." She looked at the woman again. Nervous hands, roving eyes. Hypochondriac, following nurses around? She'd change her clothes the next time she came out. The uniform showed under the coat, the white shoes.

"I saw you leave the house. I was sitting in the park .... I used to know Mrs. Manson slightly. How is she?"

Hypochondriac with curiosity bump. "She's much better, thank you," Milly said. "Now run along," she added silently. "You make me feel as if I were under a microscope."

"I'm glad of that," the woman said quietly. "I heard somewhere that she'd had a bad relapse. I'm glad it isn't true."

"Oh, no. She's much, much better."

"I know them all," the woman went on. "Not intimately, but I know them. The Mansons, Bruce Cory, and those people next door, the Perrys. And Doctor Babcock."

Milly shifted uneasily. There was too much emotion under the quiet voice. Is she trying to tell me something? she wondered. Or does she want me to tell her? Suddenly she remembered the anonymous customer in her friend Marge's book store, the woman who'd tried to buy information about Milly with a ten-cent greeting card. Finish this as soon as you decently can, she told herself, and move on.

"I'm sorry I don't know your name." The woman's smile was stiff and strained. "It seems rude to be talking to you without knowing. But mine is Byrd. B-y-r-d. I live in New York, but I often come out here because it's so pretty." As she talked, she watched Milly's face. "Byrd," she repeated. "Miss Byrd."

Milly smiled and said nothing.

"Is Emma well? I know Emma, too."

"Emma's fine."

A bus lumbered to the stop, and Milly looked at her watch. "Glendale bus, that means it's—golly, I've got to run." She got up.

Miss Byrd took her arm. "I'd appreciate it if you'd—what I want to say is—Miss—Miss—if you'd give me just a minute of your time!"

"I'm awfully sorry, Miss Byrd, but I'm due at my mother's. See you again sometime." She ducked into the crowd that surged toward the bus, crossed the street, and walked rapidly in the wrong direction for home. Miss Byrd looked like the kind of woman who'd compromise on a nurse's mother.

Marge's apartment was a few blocks farther on. She rang the bell, but there was no answer. After that she walked on small, empty side streets and bought herself a chocolate bar and a tube of toothpaste in a shabby store that smelled of kerosene.... If Miss Byrd washed her face, she might look human. But then, she might not, either. She might look—

She told herself to stop thinking about Miss Byrd. She walked on, eating the chocolate, killing time, putting off her return. What am I stalling about? she wondered. Why don't I go back where I belong?

CLIMB. You'll have to climb.

The attic door was open, the last tool clattered to the floor. Her hands were aching, they were all she could feel. Emma was behind her. Ralph and Bruce were crowding ahead of her.

"My hands hurt," she said. "Give me your hand to hold, Ralph. Brucie, give me yours. Don't leave me."

Ralph said, "Here, darling, but I wish you wouldn't—"

Bruce said, "She can't stop now."

There was a draft on the attic stairs, coming down to meet them, blowing her robe, lifting the hair from her forehead. She thought: We're wrong about this, we'll have champagne tonight in celebration of being wrong. He's writing up there, he locked the door because he hates to be interrupted, and he's dead to the world in some silly plot and can't hear us. She called his name, laughing, but no sound came out of her mouth.

Ralph said, "There must be a window open."

Bruce said: "There is. I saw it from the street."

She answered them in her mind: "You fools, of course there's a window open. The boy has to have air. It's always suffocating in that place."

The climb was endless, there had never been so many steps before. It was years before they came to the turn halfway up. Emma panted behind them. It was hard on Emma. What was? Only the stairs, that's all, the stairs. Emma was old.

Ten to one he went to sleep, she wagered silently. They give him too much to do down there at the bank, he hates figures, they wear him out. He was exhausted, and he came home early and went to sleep on that old sofa he won't let me throw away. Ten to one—Why are you saying ten to one, even to yourself? You never talk like that.... You're talking like that because you don't want to think. Well, you'd better think. Think hard, and be ashamed of yourself for even listening to their monstrous story. Monstrous? Criminal! You could sue, you could easily sue the whole lot of them for saying the things they did. Ten to one.

"Bruce," she said, "you're going too fast."

"We're crawling, Nora. You're holding us back."

"No, no! Ralph, Bruce, keep my hands!"

The attic floor was level with her eyes now. It was washed with gold from the western windows. She raised her eyes.

"What's the boy doing?" Emma's head appeared beside hers. "Robbie, you stop whatever you're doing and come straight down here!"

Robbie's shoes, above the sunny floor, were swinging in space. His brown shoes, his—he—

She went the rest of the way alone and stood before him. When she wanted to see his face, she had to raise her head, because he was hanging from the rafters.

EMMA looked up when she heard the clatter of the lunch tray. "You didn't have to bring that," she said. "I was going to ring for one of the others. You're back too soon."

"I got bored." Milly put the tray on the table.

"It looks good," Emma said. "That jelly looks good. She's a fine cook, Mrs. Perry. Maybe she'll teach you one of these days." Emma's eyes had the mating look.

"Move your workbasket, Emma. No tatting in the soup, please. Thanks. Why don't you ask me to save you a piece of wedding cake? You're slipping."

"What are you so high and mighty about?"

"I'm not." Milly slid out of her coat. "Yes, I am, and I don't know why. I hate everything. Maybe I need sleep." She walked around to the front of the chair. "Hello, there. Haven't I seen you somewhere before?"

"Bless my soul, is she awake? Must have just happened." Emma joined Milly at the chair, and they smiled steadily.

"We look nice and rested after our little nap," Emma said. "And we're going to eat every crumb and spoonful of our lunch, because if we do, then maybe we can have our lovely sherry before dinner. Can't we, Miss Sills?"

"I wouldn't know about that. I'm only the night nurse. I don't come on until seven."

Emma chortled. "Isn't she a one, Miss Nora? Aren't you a lucky girl to have Miss Sills around? I never thought I'd laugh again, not in this house. I never—" Emma caught her guilty tongue between her teeth. "Miss Nora, I—I'm going to get another lamp, and I'm the only one who knows how to do it." She hesitated at the door. "What about you? Did you have lunch at your mother's?"

"I'm not hungry. And hurry up. It'll be dark in about five hours."

Milly unfolded the heavy napkin, spread it carefully, and admired the lavish monogram. She patted the thin, still hands under the steamer rug. "Don't get wrong ideas about Emma and me," she said. "We're crazy about each other. And now let's eat whatever Hattie felt like sending up. This is beef broth, as if you couldn't see for yourself. And this is a sweetbread, as if you couldn't see that, too. And here we have the madam's jelly, shaking in its shoes. Want to start with dessert and work back, just for the—for the fun of it?"

Mrs. Manson's eyes looked steadily into hers.

She returned the dessert spoon to the tray and dropped the prattle and the professional smile. What she saw in Mrs. Manson's eyes filled her own with dismay. Mrs. Manson was looking at her from the bottom of a pit.

"Mrs. Manson?" she said quietly. "Mrs. Manson, I haven't given you what you need. I've tried, but everything I've done is only what anybody else could do. You need more than that, every day you seem to need more. It isn't only that you're sick and unhappy. I'm not very old, Mrs. Manson, but I've seen a lot of sick people, working in wards with the kind of people you never even passed on the street, never even dreamed of. And now, in the last few days, I'm beginning to see a resemblance between them and you. That's awful, Mrs. Manson, but I have to say it. You and I are friends, we both know that, and friends tell each other the truth. You're more than sick and unhappy. All day and night you live with your eyes on death, watching, waiting for —the nod. That's not right. You don't have to die. There's no medical reason for it. No reason at all unless you want to, and if that's the case, then I can't stop you. If you want to get well, you can. You're better than you were—they're not kidding when they tell you that. And you know me, I wouldn't kid you ever, not if they paid me for it. Not you, I wouldn't. You're my friend. Mrs. Manson, I want you to stop looking like that. I won't let you die if you'll help me."

Mrs. Manson's eyes closed for an instant, and her breast rose and fell as if she were climbing.

"That's better," Milly said. "And it's all right to cry. You'd been crying when I came in, but I didn't want to say anything before Emma. Golly, Mrs. Manson, I wish I knew someone who was an old friend of yours, like someone you went to school with. Someone who's your own kind. A person like that might be able to help me. A person like that could tell me what your mind is like and how you used to act when things went wrong. I've got a feeling you always act the right way, no matter what. And that scares me. It means that whatever is wrong is terribly wrong, and acting right and thinking straight can't change it."

MISS SILLS, Miss Sills, don't let anyone hear you say that. Not today, not tonight. Tomorrow you'll be safe, but not today or tonight. Don't talk to anyone until tomorrow. Tomorrow you'll be interviewed, that's when you must talk. Tomorrow, tomorrow morning…. Miss Sills, Miss Sills, there was a woman in the park. I know she could help us both, I know it in my heart. But she didn't speak, I watched and she didn't speak, and you walked by.

"I told you it was all right to cry," Milly said. "Take a look at me, it's getting to be like the common cold. There now, I'm getting fresh again and that's all right, too. No more sad talk until tomorrow. What do you want first, jelly or soup? Soup? Oke."

Emma came in with a lamp, looking like a child who has made a beautiful thing out of something nobody wanted.

Milly crowed. "Bring that thing around here, Emma. I want Mrs. Manson to see it. Glory be, and they sent the other one to the White Elephant Sale! If ever I saw a white elephant in the beaded flesh—"

"It's my own property," Emma said indignantly. "I've had it for years, and I take good care of it. I like beads."

"Where did you get it?"

"At the White—never you mind. It gives me a nice, soft light, easy on the eyes. How are we coming on?"

"Fine."

"You going out again this evening? Doctor Babcock said you could. He said you should take things easy."

"What's behind the unselfish build-up?"

"Well, I thought if you were going to be in, I might slip out for a while myself. My sister's daughter just had her first—only five pounds for all her trouble. Still and all, I thought I'd like to hear my sister brag."

"Go ahead. I don't want to go out again. And five pounds is okay, so let her brag."

"You, and not even married yet. You never did tell me where you went this morning and what you did."

"I didn't do anything, just walked. Bounced a ball with a cute kid. Oh, sure, and I got picked up, too."

"If you did, then you invited it."

"Not me, not this one. This was a woman, and she said she knew—now, now, Mrs. Manson, please."

"Maybe that spoon's too full. It looks too full to me."

"Don't rile me, Emma. She picked me up at the bus stop. She said she knew you, Emma. She asked how you were."

MISS SILLS! Emma! Emma, listen. This is what I prayed for. Listen, Emma, it's Miss Byrd, I know it's Miss Byrd. Emma, ask questions, ask—

Emma said, "I know everybody in this town, and everybody knows me and how I am." She smoothed her apron and looked at the clock. "I promised Hattie—What was the woman like?"

"Ordinary, except for her face. Too much make-up."

"Don't know her."

"Green coat and hat."

"I know seven, eight women with green coats and hats. All my friends know how I am. You might as well give up that jelly, Miss Sills. Can't you see she don't want it? I'll give it to Hattie. Well, I promised Hattie I'd take the front door and the phone while she has a rest. If you want me, ring. I'll come back later, anyway." Emma took the lunch tray when she left.

Milly tucked in the edges of the steamer rug and moved her chair beside Mrs. Manson's. Mrs. Manson closed her eyes again; it was the same as closing a door. There was nothing to do about that.

Behind Milly, the door to the hall was open and the house was as quiet as the room. The roses on the table were dropping their petals; they weren't lasting. Not the way they should. Only one day old, and they were dying.

The chair was low. From where she sat she could see the yellow trees against the sky. Now and then a leaf fell, drifting slowly as if it knew the first, lone journey downward from the sun led to the end.

It was silly to shiver in a warm room. The fire was ready for lighting if she wanted it. All she had to do was walk across the room. But it was too much trouble, too much effort. I'm tired, she thought, and why shouldn't I be? Maybe I can sleep. At least I can try. Her head dropped forward, and she sighed.

They sat side by side with closed eyes, but only one of them slept. The clock ticked on, the minutes passed, but only one of them counted.

It was after four when Doctor Babcock came in. Milly woke and saw him standing before her. She got to her feet, stumbling, only half-awake. "Doctor Babcock, I'm sorry! But Mrs. Manson seemed to be resting, and I—"

He waved her apologies aside. "A charming picture, Miss Sills, charming; and no harm done, no harm at all." His hand took one of Mrs. Manson's. "Any change? I'm afraid we're in a state of depression."

She stood behind Mrs. Manson's chair and nodded. He was a fool to talk like that where she could hear.

He went on "But that's to be expected—yes, we expected that. And Emma says there's an aversion to food."

"I wouldn't call it that I think she does very well, considering Doctor Babcock, if it's warm tomorrow, can I wheel her out on the porch?"

He thought it over "Not yet, Miss Sills. This lovely room, the sanctuary of four walls—I think we'll be happier here. The outdoors is sometimes—frightening."

Since when? Milly answered silently. Put them out in the sun and air as soon as they can sit up, that's the way I heard it. "Yes, Doctor Babcock," she said.

Doctor Babcock left Mrs. Manson and made a slow tour of the room, examining everything small enough to handle. Even Emma's workbasket was looked into. Milly adjusted the rug again and whispered to Mrs. Manson. "The way he's looking at things, you'd think he was going to put us up at auction."

Doctor Babcock made another turn around the room and came to a stop behind Mrs. Manson's chair. "Miss Sills," he said, "I'm distressed. About you. I'm not happy about you, not at all happy. You're beginning to show the strain. Now, I want you to understand that this is no reflection on your capabilities, but I truly believe you need assistance, or even better than that, a little rest."

"No, I don't," Milly said. "I mean, thank you, but I'm not tired and we don't want another nurse. Mrs. Manson and I get along fine, we're used to each other, we can practically talk. You

COMPOSITION FOR FOUR HANDS

don't want anybody else, do you, Mrs. Manson? See, she says no. That look means no. She says you're very kind, Doctor Babcock, but Miss Sills is my one and only dream girl and she's all I need." A fine line to give the boss, she mourned; every word a step home to mother, and sitting by the phone all day waiting for a call to take care of more tonsils. "But whatever you say, Doctor Babcock. I only mean—"

He smiled broadly. "No explanations, my dear. I understand. We'll wait and see how things develop. Now, about Emma. I've suggested to Emma that she sleep in her own bed tonight. I don't want Mrs. Manson relying too much on Emma. Someone unconnected with the past, a stranger like yourself, a—dream girl, did you say? Ah, yes, a dream girl is what we need!" His laughter filled the room.

No tonsils today, she decided. "Any instructions, Doctor Babcock?"

"No. Everything as usual."

When he left, she returned to her chair beside Mrs. Manson. She studied the pale face and closed her eyes until Emma came. It was four-thirty then.

Emma lighted the fire, and they both sat before it. Mrs. Manson had shown no interest in the fire; she'd looked at it once and closed her eyes again.

"We'll leave her where she is," Milly said softly to Emma. "It's the only privacy she has, sitting off by herself like that. It's all right for a little while."

Emma held her hands to the blaze. "I've got the blues," she whispered. "I can't get Robbie out of my mind. He's been walking behind me all day."

"Is today anything special?" Her own voice was low.

"No, just a Sunday. He was always around all day Sunday, running up-and downstairs, slamming doors. Hattie says she heard him last night."

"Hattie's crazy. You said so yourself."

"I know I did. And so she is. But—"

Milly looked over at the chair. "Are you awake, Mrs. Manson?" She turned back to Emma. "No, this time she's really asleep. She never tries to fool me, she knows she can't. We can talk if we're careful, you know .... Robbie. I don't know much about Robbie. George keeps changing the subject, and the papers were careful not to say more than they had to."

"They always do that when it's money and banks and prominent people. But she paid up, every cent. There's no reason you shouldn't know about it. Nobody lost a penny through us. We paid."

She could hardly bring herself to believe it even now, Emma said. "Robbie was spoiled, we know that. But why would he steal a lot of money that he didn't need or even spend? Nobody could ever prove that he spent a penny more than his regular income. Why would he steal money, then, and where did it go? Not so much as a nickel ever showed up."

What's more, she said, they'd never been able to find a single person who'd ever seen him in the wrong kind of company. No gambling, no horse racing, no bad women. There was no sense to it, none at all, and as for what he did afterward—

EMMA described what she knew of Robbie's last day. "He came home while I was at the stores," she said. "I'd have spotted something wrong if I'd been home and seen him. But I was at the stores, and Hattie had the kitchen door shut and didn't hear him come in. And when I came back, I started to work right away. I was busy phoning for the extra things Miss Nora wanted for a special dinner. She was counting on Mr. Brucie to come. I was planning a wonderful dinner, like she wanted, and then they told me."

Her tremulous whisper led Milly step by step. They stared into the fire as Emma filled the hall with running feet, crouched before the attic door, and emptied the dusty tool chest on the floor. They heard the doorbell ring above the sound of tools.

"Mrs. Perry was calling," Emma said, "and the man with the pheasant, because Hattie was afraid to open the back door. That pheasant was in the icebox for over a week—we had to give it away.... He'd written her a little note. It was in his typewriter. He said, 'I never was any good, but you wouldn't believe it.' No love or nothing. She saw it before we did—we couldn't help that. We were trying to—you know, you—you have to cut the rope.... I gave that boy the first bath he ever had."

Milly's hands went out to Emma. "Don't talk any more," she whispered. "That's enough. I know how you feel."

"You know? In a million years you wouldn't know. And it wasn't enough that I saw him as I did. I had to be the one to find her, too. Lying at my feet, the same as dead, and Mr. Ralph and Mr. Brucie out of their minds. She'd be dead this minute if it hadn't been that Doctor Babcock had come to call.... I don't know what we've done, it's like a punishment."

"Hush."

The coal crackled, the firelight was on their faces. They drew together, the bent black figure and the straight white one. On the other side of the room a shaft of setting sun came in at the window and found the chair.

HATTIE came in at five-fifteen with her plate of meat, an uncooked lamb chop and a slice of turkey breast. Her mouth was set in an obstinate line. She had clearly been told to keep it shut, and just as clearly she was going to make somebody suffer.

"That's a poor-looking chop," Emma said. She took the plate and crossed to the chair. "Open your eyes, Miss Nora, time to wake up. Hattie's here with your dinner meat, and if you want my advice, you'll take the turkey. The lamb that gave that chop could ill afford to spare it."

Mrs. Manson looked at the plate. For the first time, she seemed unwilling to play their little game.

"Serve them both, Hattie," Milly said. "Two dinner trays, one for me, too. We'll decide which we want then. It's all right, isn't it, if I eat up here tonight?"

"No reason why you can't," Emma said. She bustled to the door. "Come along, chatterbox. I'll bring up that sherry, too, Miss Sills. A nip of sherry, a nice fire—Hattie!"

The sun was low in the sky; long shadows came into the room. Milly moved aimlessly from window to porch door, from door to bed to fireplace. Once she returned to the bed, for no reason that she knew. She smoothed the covers as if she were removing the outline of a body, not preparing to receive one.

The room slowly filled with dusk, but she ignored the lamps. She sat by the fire, wondering if the radio would bother Mrs. Manson if she played it softly. There was a radio within reach of her hand; she stretched out her hand, but let it fall almost at once. Nothing she could think of was worth doing.... I used to like the autumn, she thought, but this year it's different. It used to be full of—I don't know, promise or something—but this time I feel old, and I'm not old. Tonight I'm so old that I can't look forward. I can't think of anything I want, and I've always wanted something. Now that I don't want anything, what's the use?

She looked at the still figure, shrouded in dusk. Sleep, she said to herself, sleep, Mrs. Manson. You think too much when you're awake, I know. Those attic stairs—Emma says they're dreadful. How could she do it? ...

Miss Sills, Miss Sills, go home, Miss Sills. It's growing dark. Your mother has a house; go there. All day I've seen the night getting ready. The things that could have held it back—Hattie, the lamp, Miss Byrd—are gone. Go home, Miss Sills. Miss Sills, so young and so wise, leaning forward to look into my face, telling me how frightful life can be. Little Miss Sills, my friend, go home. You don't know what comes and goes in this house ....

One by one the others drifted in, Mr. Manson, Bruce Cory, George. There were no highballs this time; they seemed to know that talk and laughter were out of place this time. This time.

Milly offered chairs, but they were declined. Someone turned the radio on, and the soft, invoking voices of a Negro choir filled the dusky room. *Abide with me: fast falls the eventide.* The voices and the dark together were unsupportable.

"Turn that off," Milly heard herself say. "I don't like it." She was startled by the sound of her voice. It cracked like a whip. "It's gloomy," she said defensively. Some tactless fool, she thought. If I knew which one, I'd give him what for.

The music stopped. George walked around the room, turning on lights. Bruce Cory said, "I'm sorry, Miss Sills."

Why did I do that? she wondered. *Miss Sills, this is no reflection on your capabilities, but you're beginning to show the strain.*

Mr. Manson said: "I'm afraid we came at a bad time. Is anything wrong?"

"No, Mr. Manson. I guess we're tired, that's all. It's been a tiring day."

"We'll go. Babcock was here, wasn't he?"

"Yes, he was. But he didn't say anything in particular. He stayed only a little while."

"Cory and I went into town for an hour or so. I wish I'd— well, we'll get along and let you rest. Anything you want, Miss Sills? You don't make many demands. I wish you did."

"No, sir, I don't want anything."

They left, Manson and Cory, but George stayed.

"Come out on the porch," George whispered. "You can, can't you? I want to talk."

THE garden was dark; across the autumn grass, patched with fallen leaves, the Perrys' lights gleamed through the trees. Mr. Perry was working on his side of the hedge, a stooped, black figure in the stream of yellow lamplight, curiously alone. "His flowers," George said vaguely. "Come along this way." He led her to the far end of the porch. She knew Hattie's room was directly beneath them.

"I've got the wind up," George said.

"Same old wind you're always talking about? I didn't come out here for that."

"Milly, listen. I'm not kidding. There wasn't any wind last night. That lamp didn't blow over; it couldn't. It was knocked over, by you or Emma or somebody else. And I don't mean Mrs. Manson, either. Do you think Emma did it?"

"No. She'd tell everybody right away and start paying off, week by week. And it wasn't me. You make me feel funny, and I was bad enough before."

"Listen. I prowled around here at the crack of dawn, also before I came in just now. I was looking for prints. I wasn't sure that what I saw last night was a dog. It ran on all fours, but it was too big. If it was a cat burglar making a fancy getaway, then we ought to tell the cops. And if it was a dog, we ought to tell them just the same. A dog that walks into second-floor bedrooms and knocks over fifteen-pound lamps ought to be tied up—or shot."

Milly rested her arms on the railing and looked down into the dark tangle of ivy. There was a light in Hattie's window. The ivy was broken; she could see the loose, limp rope of leaves and stem.

"I know that poem, too," she said slowly. "I can even quote a different line."

"You're catching on," he said. "But let me. I do it prettier 'Are you a beast of field and tree, or just a stronger child than me?' "

They drew together; his hand was on her shoulder, her face was close to his.

"George," she whispered, "where were you at ten-thirty last night?"

"Bed. Why?"

"I called you up from home, but nobody answered."

"I heard the phone, but I didn't do anything about it .... I've got you close, Milly. Don't shiver."

"Who's shivering? You haven't said anything about finding prints."

"I found some, all right. Of shoes, men's shoes. Manson and Cory were out there this morning with Babcock. Their prints are all over the place now."

"But you didn't see anything the first time—I mean, at the crack of dawn? You didn't, George, did you?"

HE WAS a long time answering. His hand left her shoulder and pressed her cheek. "I'm going down to the barracks and talk to Ferd Pross. There was something funny going on around here last night. Ferdie will know what to do."

"George, you did see something! What was it?"

"Something stood in the flower bed under Hattie's window, either before or after climbing the ivy. The same thing that got into Mrs. Manson's room. It was frightened off—my guess is the lamp—and I don't know where it went. But at one time during the night it stood in soft, wet earth, ran along the porch, swung over the railing, and tore the ivy. That's one of the things I'm going to tell Pross."

"What—what's the other?"

"It left the wrong kind of tracks. Wrong for an animal, wrong for a man. They were spaced as an animal's would be, four nice clear prints, front and back. And big. Maybe I ought to laugh, but I don't feel like it. Because they weren't feet, and they weren't paws. They were hands."

She heard herself say, "Hands?"

"Yeah." He went on, softly. "So: 'Are you beast of field and tree, or just a stronger child than me?' If that's some guy's idea of a practical joke, Ferdie and I can act funny, too. Of course they aren't there now; they got stepped on this morning. Ferdie may try to tell me I'm crazy, but I'm not."

"George, what did they look like? Were they—like a starfish?"

He said, "How did you know that?"

She quoted Hattie. "But she said only *one*."

"That can be all right, that can still make sense. It could have been reaching down to get a grip or a foothold. When she yelled, it swung back to the porch, out of sight. Then when she left, it dropped to the flower bed and vanished. Don't ask me where or how. One set of prints was all I could find. Maybe it floated."

"I'm not afraid," she said.

"No reason to be. A dirty trick by some heel whose mind didn't grow as fast as his body. Just keep the door locked. I'm pretty sure that was a one-night stand." He kissed her briefly. "This is no time for prolonging pleasure. I've got to get down to see Ferdie. Maybe somebody else saw the thing and reported it. Maybe Ferdie will hang around here tonight." He kissed her again. "Maybe I'll drop in myself."

He had reached his side of the hedge when a sudden recollection made him stop and look back at the house he had just left. *You need two pairs of hands around here.* Who said that? When? Hattie? No, Emma. This morning. Emma. That was right, but it wasn't enough. It was older than that, it went farther back. Two pairs of hands. Now, what does that—

His mother was in the living room, knitting. "Well?" she asked.

"No dinner for me," he said. "I've got to see a man about a dog."

"Knowing you, dear," she said thoughtfully, "I suspect that's vulgar."

It was six-thirty when Emma brought two dinners on a large tray. Emma and Hattie had surpassed themselves, but Mrs. Manson wouldn't eat. Milly cajoled, begged, and threatened, but Mrs. Manson refused to open her mouth. Even the sherry, which she ordinarily liked, brought no response. When they saw it was useless, they put her to bed. She fought that, too, if it could be called fighting. The mutiny was in her eyes. It was the same look Milly had seen the night before when she'd refused the hot milk and the sleeping pills.

"You run along, Emma," Milly said. "Maybe she'll change her mind when she sees me eating."

After several half-hearted offers to stay, Emma agreed to go. "If you want anything, ring for Hattie; but don't expect any conversation—she's still not talking. And she knows my sister's telephone number, in case, which I hope not."

Milly ate her dinner with elaborate and false enjoyment, and drank a glass of sherry. Mrs. Manson watched without expression. When the tray had been placed in the hall and the fire built up, there was nothing else to do. Emma's lamp shed a dim light on the bed and the inevitable steamer rug. The porch door was closed, and so was the door to the hall. The room was too hot, but Mrs. Manson liked it that way; at least, they thought she did. They thought, they thought, they thought. Would there ever come a time when anyone knew what she wanted?

Milly went to the window seat and huddled on the cushions like a child, with her arms around her knees. The lights across the park looked far away.

EMMA has gone, and Miss Sills is asleep. Curled like a kitten, her head in her arms. How long will it be before she wakes? How long before Emma comes home? One hour? Two?

Emma. Does it mean anything that Emma is out? Each time, Emma was out. Each time the house was empty except for Hattie, in the kitchen with the door closed. Except for Hattie and me and—

Why does my body ache? Perhaps because it is fighting or because I'm thinking of the last time it was alive.

Why did I go up there the last time? If I hadn't gone, I'd be living tomorrow. I'd be walking tomorrow, riding, driving, going to the theatre. My heart would be empty, but I'd be living, and perhaps in time someone else would have learned what I learned. In time to do something. Someone else, even a curious stranger; it couldn't have stayed hidden forever.

Why did I go up there? You know why. You went because you always turned the knob; every time you passed, you turned the knob slowly and quietly, knowing the door would be locked, but turning the knob because you had to. And that time the door opened.

And you told yourself you were alone in the house!

It's all right, it's all right. This is preparation of a kind, too. Climb again ....

THE knob turned soundlessly, and the door swung open. She stood at the foot of the winding stairs, looking up, listening to the soft footfalls above. Someone else had found the unlocked door.

Hattie? No, Hattie was in the kitchen or in her own room. Emma? Emma had gone to market; she'd seen her less than ten minutes ago, haggling over fish. Ralph? Brucie? Brucie had promised to come out. No, too early for them. They were in town, at the bank.

Someone who knew their daily plans and schedules had broken in. She was supposed to be at the Civic League meeting, but the pity in the other women's faces had driven her home.

She started up the stairs, shaking with fury, not fear. Robbie's attic, his own place, his last place on earth. She moved without sound, hugging the wall, hesitating only once, asking herself what she would do or say when she reached the top. She told herself she ought to call the police. I ought to call the police but I don't want—I don't want the story in the papers. They'll reprint the pictures, they'll—

Why don't I go to my room first and see if he's taken anything? If he has, I'll tell him he can keep it. I won't prosecute. I'll reason with him. I'll tell him to go, go quickly. I'll explain how we feel about the attic.

But if he has my jewelry, why did he go to the attic?

Hattie. It must be Hattie, looking for extra blankets. It has to be Hattie.

Then she heard the laughter, low, almost bubbling, happy, victorious, and familiar. She covered her mouth with her hand and crept forward.

At the top of the stairs she crouched behind the partition. There was sun on the floor again. Robbie's old toy trunk, filled with broken treasures, had been brought from its corner, and it was open. Herself unseen, she watched the hands as they lifted the packages one after the other, lovingly. There was no look of surprised discovery on the face. It was the face of one who had returned to gloat.

She stood erect. "Thief," she said quietly.

The answering voice was as quiet as hers. "This is unfortunate."

Neither moved. They looked at each other over the open trunk. A golden bar of sunlight slanted through the western window and fell between them, a metaphoric pale that placed the other one beyond the limit of civilized mercy and protection.

When she could force herself to look down again, she saw that the money in the trunk was incredibly green. The building blocks were drab and dull beside it, the once-bright trains and trucks, the painted wagons, and the battered wooden animals were ghosts. The money was real.

She said: "I misjudged you. I didn't know you had the mind for a thing like this. I thought you were reliable and capable. I even thought that you lacked imagination. I didn't know you could plan and execute a thing like this. Did you do it alone, or did someone help you? I can't understand how you did it alone."

"No imagination? Yes, everyone thinks that. Dull and pompous. Yes, I did it alone. I've always been underestimated."

"Why did you do it?"

"Because I like money, and I don't like rich women who inherit theirs. Because my own efforts never got me quite enough of my own. I thought a secret nest egg would be very pleasant, doubly pleasant when I found I could arrange it with complete safety to myself. I still think so."

She told herself to wake up. She spoke aloud, but didn't know it. "Why don't you wake up?" she said. "Why doesn't somebody wake me up?" She looked from the face to the trunk again. There were splashes of brilliant yellow among the clean greens and faded blues and reds.

SHE said, "He made those—for Christmas, I think. He made them for a joke, like a stocking toy. They were supposed to be funny. You think they're funny now, don't you? I don't. I—" She put her hands to her head. "I'm the dull one," she said, "but then, I never had to be anything else. I never had to worry about anything, or work to live. There was always someone to take care of me and do my thinking for me. But now I want to think for myself."

"Don't."

"But I want to know how you did it. I used to hear people talk about the way we managed the bank. They used to laugh and say it looked wide open, that the Board of Directors and even the watchmen thought they could go anywhere and carry off anything—until they tried."

"It wasn't difficult. I'm capable and reliable. You said so yourself."

"You are also— You killed him."

"I did."

"Why? Wasn't there anyone else you could use?"

"There may have been. I didn't look very far. He was there; he was made to order. That's how it started. Then he had the effrontery to spot me, *me,* the last person in the world they'd have thought of! So I had no choice. He had Cory blood—the inquisitive, shrewd, banker blood. He'd taken me in completely. I didn't know he could even add. Fortunately, he couldn't hide his feelings, and I saw the end in time. So I did a little talking in the right places."

"That's what was wrong with him at lunch. He wouldn't tell me then." She could have been standing before a counter of merchandise, accepting and rejecting. One finger lay along her cheek. I will not scream, she thought, I will not scream, not yet, not for days and days. I will not scream now.

"That's why he came home early," she went on. "To tell me the truth. He had been openly accused, and he knew—"

"Don't burden yourself with details. They don't matter."

She thought that over. They don't matter. The details don't matter. Why don't they? I know, I know why. Because I won't have any use for them. I'm to kill myself like Robbie; disgrace and shame will make me follow my son. Mrs. Ralph Manson, of Larchville, whose son— "You don't know me," she said.

"No?" The low laugh bubbled up again.

She pretended not to hear it. She took a step backward—a small, unnoticeable step. "Tell me one thing more," she said. "Didn't he—defend himself?"

"Oh, yes. That surprised me. I'd always thought of him as a spoiled brat, without stamina. But he was no coward."

"Thank you. You see, some of the details do matter, after all. And the open window? I wonder now why you didn't close it. Wasn't that—dangerous for you? He might have cried out."

"You're underestimating me again. I opened the window afterward. You know, you're taking this almost too well, so I'll give you the rest of it. Bodies stay warm. In a place like this, he would have been warm for an uncomfortable length of time—for me. So I opened the window to—you understand?"

"Yes, I understand. Haven't we all been stupid? You came in the front door?"

"Certainly. You've also been stupid about that, leaving it unlocked to save your servants. I made sure, of course, that there was no one in sight."

"It's only unlocked in the afternoons," she explained carefully. "I always thought that afternoons, in a place like this—I'm glad it was you who typed that note."

"I thought it was a good note, under the circumstances. I'm not much of a writer. He could have done a better job himself, but we didn't have time for that. And speaking of time, there isn't much of it left now."

"No," she agreed. "Emma will be coming soon. I saw her in the market, and she knows I'm home."

There was tolerant curiosity behind the soft voice. It was more human than the fresh peal of bubbling laughter. "I'm glad she knows you're in the house alone. But how, exactly, do you think that can help you?"

"Help me? Emma? I don't need Emma for what I'm going to do. I'd rather she didn't come. This is all mine."

"Wait. What do you think you're going to do?"

"I'm going to the police. I'm going to hang you higher than that rafter."

The air churned. Between her and the sun a human, black projectile rose and catapulted forward. She closed her eyes when it struck.

When her body rolled against the wall at the turn in the stairs, like a log jammed in midstream, she knew she hadn't long to wait. Strong hands turned her over and sent her the rest of the way. A thin scream came from nowhere.

SHE opened her eyes to nothing. After an endless search she saw a lighted lamp in another world. Soon it became familiar; it was her lamp, her room. Her bed.

Living, she told herself. Why?

Voices drifted through the gloom, like recorded voices on an old record. Thin, without bodies. But when she tried, she could see bodies standing in a row at the foot of the bed.

"At my feet, on the floor, at my feet. I came in, and I heard a sound, and I ran. I knew where it came from. Unconscious, I said to myself, or dead."

"Lucky for us that we happened to be—"

"She should be dead. She should be dead. I don't understand it."

"I've been afraid—"

She was lying at the foot of the attic stairs again, hearing Emma scream in the lower hall, looking up at the figure bending above her, reading the eyes that looked down into hers, watching the quick retreat to the top of the stairs so that whoever came— Forget that now, she told herself. Listen to the voices, listen to every word. One of them will tell you what you must do.

"Shock and paralysis. I beg your pardon, you were saying?"

"She telephoned, she told me to come as soon as I could. I thought she was ill. When I came, she asked me to wait while she went upstairs. After a while I followed. I was uneasy, disturbed—"

Who said that? Who? Listen.

"And the attic door was open. Obviously she'd found the key. She was preparing to take her life in the same way. I struggled with her, she was demoralized, raving. She fell. When I heard Emma and the rest of you, I—"

Liar, her mind said. Thief, murderer, liar. You flung me like a sack of meal, but the others came and you couldn't finish. Wait until I tell them that.

"At my feet. Lying there on the floor. Oh, Mr. Ralph, Mr. Brucie!"

"Quiet, please. Miss Byrd?"

"Yes, Doctor Babcock?"

"A close watch for the next five hours. At the slightest change, call me."

"All of us will watch. Babcock, it was Providence that you were—"

"Providence? Not at all. The dear lady had been on my mind, I felt that a little call—But I must warn you, this will be a hopeless vigil. She will live from hour to hour—perhaps."

"Will she talk to us before she—"

"There will be no speech, no movement."

"No speech?"

"We'll get another opinion, we must. You understand how we—"

"Naturally another opinion. I was about to suggest it myself. Mr. Cory, not too close, please. When and if consciousness returns, she must see no one—strange."

"Strange? I? But she'll expect to see me, she knows I'm here, she asked me—"

The voices faded, the figures melted away.

So that's the story!... She could feel the bitter laughter in her throat. Wait until I tell mine. Not now, in a little while. When I'm alone with someone who will believe me.

Why aren't my bones broken? Perhaps because I didn't fight. Why don't I feel pain? They said I should be dead. Yes, I should be. I would be if the others hadn't come when they did. I will be, unless I tell. They said no speech, no movement. That's not true, either. I can talk and I can move. I—

It's true.

THE light from Emma's lamp was a dim pool on the bed table. In it were the bottle with its four pills, the vacuum jug, a clean, folded handkerchief, the jar of talcum powder. Undisturbed, still in the same positions.... No one has come while I've been away, she thought. It's too early. Is the door locked?

Miss Sills' cap is white against the dark window. Her stiff white skirt, her square-toed white shoes. Small, square white shoes like a summer Sunday morning. Sunday School. Clean them with the shoe white; you can do that yourself. Now wipe the edges of the soles—no, no, not with the sponge, there's too much whitener on the sponge. Use the cloth, that's what it's for. Stand them on the window sill, one behind the other; they'll dry in no time at all .... I never spoiled a child in my life.

The door to the hall is closed, the door to the porch is closed. Miss Sills and I are closed in. The doors may be locked from the outside, we may be locked in. The door to the hall—

The door to the hall opened.

She watched the white figure emerge from the shadows on silent feet. It had no face. It was covered with white. Two arms reached down to her.

Miss Sills.

Miss Sills said: "Hey! Sorry. But what's the big idea? Why the pussyfoot, why the disguise?"

He said something through the mask.

"Sure," Miss Sills said. "That's sensible. I didn't mean to yell at you, but I was only half-awake. I don't mind admitting you scared the—you scared me for a minute. I thought we had Martians." Miss Sills went to the bed and turned back the covers. She bent down. "He frightened you, too, didn't he? That's a shame. I should have stayed over here. But it's all right, it's all right now. You really did frighten her. Take that thing off, and come out in the open for a second. See, Mrs. Manson? It's only Breitman."

Only Breitman.

"He has a cold, Mrs. Manson. He caught it last night when he left here. He's only taking precautions for your sake. He'd just as soon scare you to death, but he draws the line at a sneeze."

Only Breitman.

HE TALKED to Miss Sills while he worked; she couldn't hear all he said. Miss Sills stood at the foot of the bed, her cap awry, her stiff skirt wrinkled where her arms had hugged her knees. She watched him and laughed with him. He wore a wrist watch. It said eight-thirty.

When he was through, he went to the fire, and Miss Sills gave him a glass of sherry from the bottle that was still on the mantel. He slipped the mask under his chin when he drank. Miss Sills laughed again. She knew Breitman; they had worked together before. Breitman was the best masseur in the business, she said.

When Breitman left, Miss Sills followed him to the door. She sounded as if she were sorry to see him go. Miss Sills was lonely, she liked people, she liked life around her.

After Breitman left, Milly went to the end of the hall and looked down the main stairs. The lower hall was dim. She crossed to the head of the kitchen stairs. No light or sound there, either. Hattie had gone to bed. Or slipped out. Usually on Sunday nights Hattie moaned hymns with the door open.

They're getting mighty casual around here, she complained to herself. You'd think they'd tell me when they go out; you'd think they'd ask me if I wanted anything. She returned to the room, rinsed Breitman's glass, and looked for something to do.

There was nothing in Emma's work-basket, no mending or darning, only the tatting, which looked so effortless in Emma's hands and turned into a cat's cradle in her own. Even Mrs. Manson was all right. Mrs. Manson was taking one of her little jaunts into another world; she was seeing something far away, far away and high up. Maybe a mountaintop; she'd traveled a lot in Europe. Well, whatever it was, there was peace in her eyes. Peace, or something just as good. There was no fright.

She went to the porch door and rested her forehead on the cool glass. No lights over at the Perrys'. Half past nine. They couldn't be in bed. Gone to the movies. Mr. Perry liked movies. George said he liked the tough ones. George said that sometimes when the old man thought he was alone with his flower beds, he flattened his back against the hedge and made like standing against a warehouse wall. Fist in pocket, making like a gun. A lookout. The old man was cute, poor thing. Acting tough all by himself and saying, "Yes, dear," the rest of the time.

Maybe George was with Ferd Pross, the State Trooper. He and Ferdie had gone to Boys' High together. He could tell Ferdie anything and know he wouldn't be laughed at. George was up in the air, all right; he couldn't fool her. And so am I, she admitted, and I'm not fooling myself either.... Why doesn't George talk to Manson and Cory? Maybe he has; maybe they're doing something about it this minute.

She was suddenly relieved. That's why they're out, she decided. That's why they didn't say anything to me. They didn't want me to know they were worried.

She went to the fire. It was burning itself out. Nearly ten o'clock. It would last until bedtime, until Emma, came back.

She sat in Emma's chair, and planned a spring offensive against George's mother, the whole thing to take place in the Sills' back garden, which was big enough and had two dogwood trees. Let's say the first of May, and no veil—I'd feel like a fool in a veil after this cap. No bouquet; let the dogwood handle that. A white prayer-book and high heels, even if I do fall flat on my face. And Mrs. Manson in her chair, under the trees. With me. Beside me. Mrs. Manson will give me away. Oh, oh, trouble ahead. Now listen, Mother, I've been everything a daughter should be. I hate to talk like this, but you force me. And I do think that, on this day of all days, you might at least try to understand and have a little consideration. Who am I fighting with? What's all the rush? ... Maybe I'd better tell George.

SHE was almost sorry when Emma came in at eleven. By that time everything had been settled but the chicken salad; veal or no veal.

"Hello," she said. "Have a nice time?"

Emma said: "It's blowing up outside, a nasty, damp fog all over. I hate it. But you're cozy enough in here. You sound real happy, too."

"That's the voice that breathed o'er Eden."

"Whatever that may be. Well, I just looked in for a minute. I'm going down to my bed. I'm beginning to feel my neuralgia. That fog. Will you be going down yourself, for hot milk?"

"I don't know." They looked at the bed. Mrs. Manson's eyes were closed. "If she stays like that, I won't. Better not to start anything."

"Well, if you do, don't lock up. They're still out. No trouble?"

"Breitman got himself up in a mask, because he's playing with the idea of influenza. Frightened her at first, the big gorilla. But aside from that, everything's fine."

"George come over?"

"No. Haven't seen a soul."

"Well—" Emma opened her handbag. "Your mother sent you a note." She drew out an envelope and gave it to Milly.

"My mother? But how did she know—"

"Sent it to my sister's. My sister's boy took it. Don't be so fussy. You've got it, haven't you? Well, I'm for bed. Be sure you ring if you want me." Emma was still talking when she closed the door.

Milly stared at the envelope in her hand. The address was lettered in pencil: "THE NURSE. KINDNESS OF EMMA. PERSONAL." She took it to the lamp by the bed. Mrs. Manson was watching her.

"So you're curious, too?" Milly said. "You don't miss much, do you?" She held the envelope before Mrs. Manson's eyes. "That's not from my mother, and you know it as well as I do. Emma's out of her mind. Well, there's only one way to find out. May I sit on the edge of your bed, madam, if I promise not to bounce? ... Well, what do you know, there's something in it. Feels like money, like a quarter or something." She opened the envelope and took out a key. "Look!" she marveled. She held the key to the light before she put it on the bed table. "Wait till I read it, then I'll tell you."

The note also was in pencil. Across the top of the first page a sentence in capital letters said: "DO NOT BEAD THIS UNLESS YOU

ARE ALONE." She winked at Mrs. Manson. "This is going to be good. Wait."

She read to herself, frowning, engrossed; she forgot Mrs. Manson. She was alone with the crackling paper in her hand.

"I WON'T sign my name to this, but you will know who I am. I said you had a good heart. There is something wrong in that house. I know it. It isn't a thing I can take to the police, because I haven't proof of anything, only what you might call my convictions. Too many things have happened in that house, and those people are not the kind that have such things happen to them. Also, I cannot go to the police because they would have to take my name, and then if they investigated and found nothing, my name would leak out, and that would be the end of me. Even now I think somebody watches my apartment at night.

"Once I knew a lady who feared for her life, I don't mean myself, and people thought she was imagining things, even the police thought she was. But it was proved that she wasn't. Your patient has the same look this other lady had. That's what I mean.

"It is not my wish to get you into trouble or danger, but I've no one else to tell this to. I couldn't find out your name, because I was afraid my interest would become known to the wrong person. I'm not sure who the wrong person is.

"This key fits the attic door. It was made from an impression. Never mind how I came by it. Now, this is why I'm sending it to you. Every time there is no one in the house but the patient and her nurse, and maybe the cook in the kitchen, somebody walks in the attic. I've heard them, because my hearing is very acute, even when they walked softly. Sometimes in daylight, sometimes at night. The patient has heard it, too. She knows what it is, but she can't tell you. That's when she has the same look as the other lady I told you about."

Milly turned the page with a shaking hand. It was ridiculous, it was crazy. It could be true. She read on.

"I couldn't use the key myself. I never had a chance. Never mind why I never had a chance—just let us say I came into possession too late. But if you know someone you are sure of, give the key to them. And tell them to be careful. Tell them to watch everybody, to trust nobody. But go to the attic.

"Maybe someday I will see you again. You didn't think much of me, I could see that; but I don't blame you. I've been half out of my mind and very nervous and not myself. But you'll understand that later.

"I remain, Your Friend."

She folded the letter and put it in her pocket. "Mrs. Manson," she said, turning slowly, "do you mind if I—*Mrs. Manson!*"

Mrs. Manson didn't hear.

One of Mrs. Manson's arms was uncovered. One hand was inching forward through space, the fingers opening and closing, taking handfuls of air, curling around the air, holding it, letting it go. The hand crept on until it reached the bed table and dropped. It struck the lid of the powder jar; the lid spun on the rim of the table and fell soundlessly to the carpet. The jar overturned.

"*Mrs. Manson.*" Milly's voice was a whisper.

Mrs. Manson's hand covered the key. Her mouth twisted and stiffened and relaxed. Her eyes met Milly's. I can't talk, her eyes said, but this is the smile you've been waiting for. Her eyes blazed and talked.

"Don't," Milly said. "Don't try. Let me. Mrs. Manson, do you know who sent that key? It's the other nurse, isn't it?"

It was.

"Do you know what she means? She says it's a key to the attic. I know it is—you've proved that. But do you know what she wants? She wants someone to go up there, she says you—"

There was no need for more. Mrs. Manson's eyes blazed their verification.

"Shall I go? Shall I go now? There's no one home."

Mrs. Manson tried to say yes, but fear and pity struggled with frenzied hope; the fear and pity and hope were as clear as printed words, clearer than speech.

"There's no one home," Milly whispered. "This is a safe time. It's better for me to go myself, now. If we wait until I call George—Mrs. Manson, we'll never sleep if I don't go now. If we wait, we might not have another chance.... But I don't know what I'm supposed to find, or see. I don't know what's there. I—"

Mrs. Manson's eyes led her to the hand covering the key. Covering the key, lying in the spilled powder.

"Mrs. Manson! Can you move one finger, can you write in that powder? Can you write even one word?"

Their breathing was like thunder in their ears. One finger. One. It moved, slowly. One word, one. The word grew, letter by letter. It was "trunk."

Milly took the key. There was a flashlight in the table drawer. She took that, too. She went to the hall door and looked at the outside lock.

"There's no key here. I can't lock you in, but I promise to hurry." She returned to the table and blotted out the word with her palm. She was smiling. "I'm going to put that hand back where it used to be, too," she said. "Just for fun. And here's my watch, right here, under the light. So you can see how quick I am, so you won't stew."

She didn't look back.

The house was still silent. The attic key was stiff in the lock, like all new keys, but the door opened without sound. She closed it behind her and climbed the stairs, following the flashlight beam.

Trunk. Trunk. What trunk? Attics are full of trunks. How will I know which one? What will I find? How will I know it's what I want, even when I see it?

She came to the top and turned her light around the room. There was a table holding a covered typewriter. There was a leather sofa with broken springs. There were cardboard boxes, hampers, discarded luggage, a dusty rocking-horse, three bicycles that told how fast a boy grows. There was a round-topped trunk with something painted on the side in large, red, crooked letters. Robbie ....

The hand crept from under the rug and found its laborious way to the table again .... Don't let anything happen, she prayed. I am on my knees. Heaven, I am on my knees. Don't make her pay for me .... The fingers curled once more. Her face was dark with pain. It would be a longer word this time.

SHE looked down into the trunk. The flashlight beam dug into the corners, picked out the colors and shapes. She saw bundles of paper money, play money for keeping store. Building blocks, trucks and trains, battered little wagons. When she took one of the bundles in her hand, she saw the money was real. She knew what it was then.

She looked from the money to the four gloves. Big cotton gloves, covered with thick bright-yellow paint, with bleeding hearts and arrows on the cuffs. She made herself take one of them in her hand. The paint was soiled and cracking, but it had been fresh and new not too long ago. At one time they had been what her mother called furnace gloves. You bought them at the five-and-ten and wore them when you did things like carrying out ashes. They were padded on the inside; two of them had room enough for hands. They were stiff and firm; the fingers were spread, but you could wear them on your hands. The other two were fastened to shoes, pulled over a pair of old shoes, filled out as if they held hands, but fastened to a pair of shoes. Like starfish.

She crept down the stairs in the dark. When she reached the hall, she heard the front door open and close softly.

Mrs. Manson watched her as she closed the room door behind her and moved a chair against the knob. Her hands left wet prints on the chair, but she didn't know that.

When she went to the bed, she said: "Don't worry about that chair. It's just a—well, it's a precaution."

Mrs. Manson's eyes questioned her steadily.

"Yes," she answered, "I saw it. Mrs. Manson, I can't use the phone. The one in here is disconnected—you know that, don't you? It was done before I came. And the others aren't safe. I won't kid you, Mrs. Manson, but don't be frightened. I'll think of something. I saw everything you wanted me to see. You saw it, too, didn't you? You went up there and saw it, too, and that was when you fell. I know you didn't fall, not like they say. But don't be frightened. It'll be all right. Ill think of something."

She left the bed and went to the porch door. She didn't open it. She dropped the latch into its slot, a flimsy latch that wouldn't keep a child out. A latch that a hairpin—

The Perry cottage was still dark. They could have come home while I was up there. It doesn't mean they're still out, just because it's dark. They could be home, in bed.

The street lamp shed a faint light along the edge of the garden, contesting the fog. There were no figures out there; no one moved along the hedges or under the trees. If Ferd Pross had agreed to watch, he hadn't come. But it wasn't much after twelve. He might think it was too early. Too early for a prowler, that's what Ferd might think.

She went back to the bed and sat down. "I have an idea," she whispered. "I'm going to turn out the lamp. You won't mind the dark, will you, if I hold your hand? This is what I mean about the dark. Last night George saw the lamp go out. Maybe he'll see it now, maybe he's watching. If he is, then maybe—"

She reached for the lamp and saw the new word cut into the film of powder. It gleamed up from the polished wood. *Murderer.*

"I know," she said. "Mrs. Manson, *can you write the name?*"

His father and mother had gone to bed; their doors were closed. George closed his own quietly and went to the window without turning on the light. Mrs. Manson's lamp was still on. So far, okay. He went to his desk and groped for a cigarette. He smoked it, sitting on the edge of his bed.

Ferd Pross hadn't laughed. He'd looked as if he'd wanted to, but not for long. They'd gone for coffee at the dog wagon, and Ferdie had listened and asked questions. He'd promised to watch the house. He'd said, "I'll do it myself, part of the time anyway, and I'll put a man on when I leave." He'd added, "If anybody but you gave me a line like this, he'd get the alcohol routine."

George had answered, "Not me, Ferd, not this time."

"What do you think it is, George?"

"I don't think. Not now. Not yet."

He went to the window again, raised it and leaned out. There was no one in sight. The fog was low on the ground; the lights along the distant street were dim; but he knew he would see Ferdie when he came.

"Give me half an hour or so," Ferdie had said. "I'll be around, front or back."

Maybe I'm sticking my neck out, George told himself. Maybe they gave all his things away. Maybe she wanted all his stuff out of the house, and they gave it to some playground outfit. Maybe some kid just happened to get hold of—

No. Not a kid, not a trick like that. An overgrown lout? ... Stop thinking with your mind closed, walk right into forbidden territory and see if you can find a way out. Now, then, suppose Robbie—

No, no, no. Wait a minute. Don't say no so quick; you've been saying no all day. To yourself. Who are you fooling? Say yes for a change, and see what you get. Suppose Robbie—

He shivered and went back for another cigarette. The first one had burned down to his fingers. When he returned to the window, the street was still empty. The garden was empty. Mrs. Manson's light—

Mrs. Manson's light went out while he watched. Out and on, out and on. Out.

By that time he almost knew the answer was yes.

He dialed the barracks on the hall phone. Pross? Pross, a calm voice said, had left. Had he said where he was going? No, he hadn't said anything, but he'd made a couple of phone calls and sounded excited.

He thought of the phone calls he would like to make, but he was afraid to use the time. But when he saw his mother standing in her doorway, he gambled with a handful of minutes.

"Listen," he said, "this is more important than it sounds. That afternoon when Robbie came home early, did you see anyone else? Anyone, *anyone.*"

"Did you wake me up for that? Is that all you can say, after staying out all night and leaving me alone with your father?"

"Please, Mother," he begged. "Quick, did you? Anyone, anyone at all."

She told him, divided between curiosity and anger. "And what's wrong with that? George, you're hurting my shoulder!"

"Sorry, sorry. Was it before or after Robbie came home?"

"A few minutes after. But why *I* should be half-killed because— *George!*"

"Stay where you are," he said. "I mean it."

THE fire was nearly dead. It was the only light; it was almost no light at all. Milly reached for Mrs. Manson's hand in the dark. "That business with the lamp was a signal," she lied softly. "I told George that if I ever wanted him, for anything, I'd do that. I wish I could see your face, Mrs. Manson. I'd like to look you straight in the eye and tell you what I think of you. I'll tell you tomorrow."

She knew they both were listening. If the porch door opens, I'll hear it, she thought. She'll hear it, too. If the hall door opens, there'll be a light along the edge, from the hall. Unless the light—

"Do you want to hear about my wedding?" she whispered. "It's going to be in the spring, and you're in it. If you want to be. I've got it all planned in my head. We'll be the talk of the town. We'll—"

She heard the latch on the porch door. Something was pressing against the glass, a dark shape.

"Mrs. Manson?" She put her lips to Mrs. Manson's ear. "I'm going to carry you. I'm going to carry you to the window seat. You'll be all right there. George will be here in a minute. No, Mrs. Manson, don't cry now. No, Mrs. Manson, not now."

The porch door opened. She stood with her back to the window seat, making a wall of her body and outstretched arms.

It swayed across the floor on all fours; she knew how it would look if the lights were on. She could hear the soft padding of the four starfish hands as they moved over the thick carpet to the bed.

She tried to kill it with her mind. She willed it to die. Beast, beast, I'm killing you.

She heard the bed shake as the body lunged.

Light burst. From the ceiling, from the hall, from the porch, it flooded the room. She was blind with light. Sound crashed and reverberated. George's voice rose above a hideous clamor. George shouted, "Ferd!" From somewhere, Ferd answered.

She began to see, then. The grappling, rolling figures on the floor began to take shape. She reached behind her and covered Mrs. Manson's eyes with her hand.

George, Ferd Pross, battered and bleeding. Babcock? Babcock and young Doctor Pleydell. How did Pleydell—

They rose and fell in a heaving mass, separating, coming together, a swollen sea of speechless men, young and old, with one objective.

Cory. Cory had a gun. George flung himself at Cory's arm. Milly gathered her strength and screamed. "No, George, no!"

The end of time had been reached when they dragged the black shape from the floor. They took away its masquerading cape. They made it stand alone and let its face be seen.

She turned and hid her own face on Mrs. Manson's breast.

She knew it was George who came to stand beside them. She knew his hand with the high-school class ring that he wore because she always made fun of it. There was powder on his hand; he saw it when she did, and he rubbed it off on his coat. She knew then that Ralph Manson's name and story were no longer written on the table.

Someone said her name softly. A new voice. "Miss Sills." She raised her head, afraid to believe. Then she cried as she had never cried before....

SHE was in her chair, in the window, waiting for morning. Morning was almost there. They had left her again, but not all of them. The ones she loved had stayed.

They said it was all right to think now. They said she could think all she wanted to. They said she could sit up all day and night, forever, if she wanted to. And think herself black in the face because she was a good, good—Stop that, she told herself. You don't have to do that any more.

That young man, the State Trooper. He was the one who'd called Babcock and Pleydell. He'd told them what he thought and asked them if his theory were possible. Medically possible, emotionally. And Babcock said he had been thinking the same way, had almost come to the same conclusion.... The Trooper said he didn't want a car for Christmas. Would a big red bow look too silly on a windshield? Ask Bruce. No, not now, later.

Bruce. Bruce had thought like Babcock. The first night had been too full of individual anachronisms. Miss Sills had been too hard to wake; not compatible with Miss Sills. The other one—she still couldn't say his name, even to herself—the other one had given too much attention to the porch door, the lamp, the litter of twigs and leaves on the floor. Bruce, trying desperately to prove himself wrong, had mapped out and timed a possible route, using the porch door as entrance and exit, starting from the rose room, allowing for the flight to the garden, the return. Then, at dinner, he'd told them all he was going into town. But he'd gone to Robbie's room and waited in the dark.... Robbie's room was the right place. Thank you, Bruce.

"Want anything?" Bruce asked now.

She shook her head. Her eyes told him she had everything. It was still hard to talk.

George Perry came in from the porch with Milly Sills. His look of confusion was not improved by his temporarily vertical hair. He bent over her chair. "What does a woman mean," he asked, "when she says 'no veal'?"